Déjà

This is a work of fiction. Names, characters, places and incidents either are the product of the author's imagination or are used fictitiously. Any resemblance to actual persons, living or dead, events, or locales is entirely coincidental.

Copyright © 2021 by James Butler

All rights reserved. No part of this book may be reproduced or used in any manner without written permission of the copyright owner except for the use of quotations in a book review.

Warning: Suicide is featured

Chapter 1

Emily Parr began to open her eyes, nothing changing very much as all which she could see was the inside of her sleeping mask and all which she could hear was the strange, silent rumble of the inside of her head, her earmuffs cancelling all sound from the world outside of her tiny bed.

It took a moment or two for Emily to fully process that she was awake as usual, blinking to rid her eyes of the dried substance which would cling to the corners of her eyes whenever she would sleep. Then, letting out a light sigh, not wanting to get up, she pulled her earmuffs from her head and slid her sleeping mask over the top of her head, the elasticated fabric which would hold it in place flicking her right, index finger, causing a light gasp of shock to escape her lips as she recoiled her right hand instinctively, gazing at her finger as if expecting a cut to have formed.

Emily placed the earmuffs and the sleeping mask on her bedside table and clambered from her bed before gazing at the vibrating phone which had fallen off of her chest and onto the mattress with the movement. As she wore earmuffs to sleep, a regular alarm wouldn't wake her. To counter that problem,

Emily set her phone to begin vibrating at the correct time, leaving it on her chest while it would charge overnight. There wasn't any chance of the phone falling off of her and, therefore, the vibrations failing to awaken her given that her bed was so small that there wasn't enough space to roll over. On the left side was a wall, on the right side was a small drop to the floor which she'd grown accustomed to avoiding while asleep.

As soon as Emily had halted the alarm, she began to pull her clothes on slowly, letting out a yawn which she tried to stifle, unsure as to whether it would make her crave to return to sleep even more than what the urge was already demanding.

It took a few minutes for Emily to climb into her work clothes, gazing at herself in the mirror for a moment, wondering if she needed to put any make-up on when she would brush her long, light-blonde hair. Emily didn't like to wear a lot of the stuff, only ever using it to conceal the occasional spot or to hide the dark circles which would sometimes appear underneath her eyes due to missing even two hours of sleep. If she wasn't going to work, was going on a date or going to visit a friend, for instance, she'd put a bit more of an effort in, though it still wouldn't be substantial. She couldn't be bothered, really, something which reflected how she felt towards a lot of things. She couldn't be bothered with school very much, passing her subjects with decent but not extraordinary grades. She couldn't be bothered with any further education, either, having jumped straight into work which she didn't like, something which she still hadn't managed to escape. She was working in a fair-sized food store, one which would have a few, large spurts of customers each day, something which she found exhausting when she wasn't prepared for it. It was a nine-to-five job, fairly standard, as she saw it, but the fact that she could get up at eight each morning as opposed to getting up at six or seven which was when her friends would usually have to get up for their jobs didn't make her feel much better about working there. It didn't matter how long she would have to work or when she would have to work, she would always stumble home exhausted.

Emily sat down at the small make-up table which resided underneath the window, just a little past the foot of her bed. It looked like there was a spot forming on her pale, left cheek. It wasn't very noticeable, but as soon as Emily had spotted it, she wanted to hide it.

A quick application of concealer dealt with the problem before she took her hairbrush and began to tackle the easily tangled, long hair which she was semi-proud of maintaining, wincing occasionally as a knot would be painful to deal with. As soon as she was done, gazing at herself in the mirror, her pale, light-green eyes scanning her smooth and somewhat-pretty face, Emily decided that she was done. She got off of the chair, grabbed her phone, and began to venture towards her kitchen in search of breakfast.

She walked out of her bedroom and into the tiny living room which, as she miserably noted as usual, was the biggest room in her apartment. The kitchen was in a corner of the living room, nothing to really separate the two areas, the right side of the fridge and the left side of the sink being where Emily considered the room to begin, a small square which wouldn't be able to fit more than six people in at a time.

Emily quickly threw some bread into the toaster and began to lean against the counter beside the toaster, checking her phone, searching for anything interesting in the news as she waited. Nothing, as usual, prompting her to switch to scrolling through the feed of one of the various social medias which she had on her phone until the toast popped out of the toaster, the noise scaring her a little, making her jump.

After spreading a small amount of butter onto the toast and dropping the two pieces onto a plate, she moved to the two-seat couch, flopping onto it, sitting upright, leaning into the left arm of the couch with her legs going to the right, pushing against the arm of the couch. She placed the small plate on the space in front of her stomach as she began to flick through the few TV channels which came for free with the device, landing on one which caught her attention before she began to eat while watching the low-budget show.

Time passed neither quickly nor slowly. Emily found herself drifting in and out of being enthralled by the show which she was watching, glancing at the clock on the wall occasionally to make sure that she wasn't losing track of time. It didn't take too long for her to decide that it was time to get to work, knowing that it would take about fifteen minutes to walk from her apartment to the shop which she worked in.

Emily slid off of the couch, placed the crumb-covered plate into the sink, went to the bathroom to brush her teeth and then walked into her bedroom to grab her coat, pulling it on and zipping it up. It was slightly cold outside, and there were a few, grey clouds in the sky, making it fairly likely that it would rain. The last thing which Emily wanted was to get wet on the way to work and then having to spend the first hour walking around in damp clothes. She simply hated the feeling of damp clothes sticking to her skin.

She left her apartment, double-checking her pockets as she walked away from the newly locked door. Phone, money, keys. All which she needed.

Emily descended the four flights of stairs, walking through the exit and onto the street, immediately feeling a light breeze. It wasn't as cold as she'd been expecting, but it wasn't exactly warm, either. It was a good thing that she'd decided to bring a coat.

She began the walk, dealing with the annoying traffic which would always seem to pile-up on the streets which she needed to cross. Given that she lived in a city and given that it was nearing nine in the morning, there were a lot of people on their way to work, resulting in bustling roads, pavements and a constant stream of irritating noise. Emily had grown-up with the loudness and busyness of the city, used to it by now, but it still bugged her sometimes. Trying to cross the road when there were at least ten cars jumping at the opportunity to drive as far as possible before the next pile-up at the traffic lights was frustrating, Emily constantly finding herself trapped on the wrong side of the road, waiting, tapping her right foot impatiently as she so often found herself doing. It was a habit which she'd picked up in high school, of few of her friends having done it, resulting in Emily having picked up the impatient gesture.

A few annoying waits and about ten minutes later, Emily could see the roof of the shop which she worked in over the top of the expanding sea of vehicles. The shop wasn't overly large, but it was big enough to see from what must have been about two-hundred metres away.

Emily crossed another road, having approached it at the perfect time to narrowly avoid another wait, stepping onto the other side of the pavement with a light, barely noticeable sigh. Getting closer and closer to the shop just made her feel as if she was going to have a rough day. She didn't know why the feeling was there, what had caused it, but there was a light buzz of dread in the back of her mind. Emily tried to ignore the feeling, trying to convince herself that she would just walk in, get her shift done, then that she would go home. That would be it. Nothing extra to add. In, shift, home.

After walking for another couple of minutes, Emily progressed through the automatic, sliding doors and immediately made her way to the back room to clock-in. On her way, she passed a colleague as he walked around in search of something. Emily didn't have much of a relationship with her peers, mainly only knowing their names and a handful of things about each of them as it was obligatory given that they worked together all of the time. Aside from knowing basic things like their names, ages and ethnicities, Emily didn't know much else. She didn't try to be very social while at work given that she was easily drained, and she especially wouldn't interact with her colleagues much if she would be manning a till and having to talk to customers very regularly. It would just take too much out of her to do so.

Emily entered the back room, made her way to the break room, then clocked-in, drawing a small tick by her name on the sheet which had been pinned to a notice board.

It didn't take very long for Emily to sink into the workday. She started off slowly, trying to get herself used to having to walk around, stock shelves, aid a few customers and occasionally having to take-over what another employee was doing when they would have to help in the check-out area. It only took what must have been an hour for Emily to be dragged to a till, a spurt of customers having entered the store; the first rush-hour.

"Have a nice day," Emily stated with a monotone voice and a forced smile to a young girl who was very clearly skipping school, not appearing to be ill and definitely not looking old enough to be considered a graduate.

Emily looked down the conveyor belt and saw that there were only two more customers to deal with before she could head to the break room and leave whoever was working on the other till to deal with the rest of the customers. It had quieted down a fair amount and, Emily knew, she needed a small break. She'd been working for at least an hour and a half without any rest, and maybe half of that time had been a little hectic. She needed a small amount of time to recharge before having to return to deal with the influx of customers searching for things to buy for their lunches.

After dropping into a chair in the break room, Emily let out a long sigh. The room was small and there were a few other people in there who had clearly had the same idea as her: to have a small break after the hectic time which they'd had during the rush-hour. Given that she wasn't exactly by herself, Emily couldn't really stretch out and take fifteen minutes off as she wanted to. Instead, she just sat there, leaning forwards, her phone in her hands as she browsed social media, lightly tapping her right foot along to the beat of a song which was stuck in her head. It wasn't the best way to spend the break, mainly because Emily couldn't sit back and take a breather, but it was good enough for her. She left the break room after two other employees had entered and another two had left, deciding that it was time to get back to work, walking back into the main area of the shop.

Emily immediately returned to stacking a few shelves, replacing items which weren't fit to be sold anymore, essentially doing chores for what felt like forever.

Lunch arrived quicker than expected, bringing another wave of customers, but that was dealt with within thirty minutes, leaving Emily to return to the break room, take a breather, then to head to the check-out as it was her turn to be the one who was responsible for the majority of the customers.

Emily sat, scanned, made light and polite small talk and was even allowed to keep a small amount of change by an older gentleman who creeped her out slightly. She could have sworn that he'd been trying to look down the neck of her shirt, but she didn't have any proof and, even if she did, she couldn't be bothered to report the behaviour.

Emily ate her lunch in the break room, taking thirty minutes away from work to do so, then returned to the floor where hours passed, though it felt as if *days* had passed, instead, Emily's tasks seeming to go on and on, taking up all of her attention which, she supposed, was a good thing. It was only when Emily's shift ended that she noticed just how much time had passed as she gleefully rushed to the breakroom to clock-out, wanting to get away from the store as quickly as possible. She wasn't going to spend a small amount of time browsing the aisles in search of a treat to buy with her employee discount as she would occasionally do after shifts, wanting something to almost congratulate herself for getting through another day of work. She just wanted to get home and to relax.

Leaving the shop felt strangely blissful. Just exiting through the automatic, sliding doors felt invigorating to Emily as she felt the light breeze which had been present for the entire day on her face, almost tickling her skin.

Emily began the walk home, crossing through the car park and then across the road, knowing that she was going to have to deal with the same thing as that morning. That was the only trouble with leaving the store right at the end of her shift; she'd have to deal with the traffic again.

It didn't take any more than a minute for Emily to have to wait for a handful of cars so that she could cross to the other side of the pavement. People were beginning to fill the pavement around her, too, showing Emily that she was probably going to have to deal with a journey which would be just as annoying as it had been that morning.

A few more minutes of walking, a few more times of having to wait for cars to move so that she could continue heading home, and Emily was starting to feel tired. That workday had taken something out of her. She just felt drained. Maybe it was because she'd gone for the last few hours without taking a break, having managed to find a rhythm of replacing items and guiding customers over and over and over and over again.

Emily closed her eyes for a moment as she walked, opening them right after letting out a light sigh.

Then something collided with the right side of her body, a force which shook her skeleton and sent her flying to the left. She'd been hit by a car!

Emily swore inside of her head, wanting to let out some type of noise, but all words felt trapped. Her brain felt fuzzy. Her body buzzed a little as if she'd been electrocuted.

Emily slammed into the concrete of the main road and barely had a second to process that another car was coming, the wheel progressing directly towards her already-bleeding head.

Chapter 2

Emily jolted awake, not seeing anything due to the sleeping mask which covered her eyes, not hearing anything due to the earmuffs which covered her ears. She was gasping for air, her chest feeling tight as she threw the earmuffs from her head followed by the sleeping mask.

She was in her room, in her bed, laying there. She'd woken up. She hadn't died.

Emily let out a long, relieved breath and felt her body go slightly limp as she relaxed into the mattress. The dream- or nightmare- had felt so real. It felt as if she'd actually died. Well, given that she didn't know what death felt like, she didn't have any frame of reference, but it felt as she'd imagined it to. She'd felt cold. Her senses had started to fail. Her body felt fuzzy as if she'd been electrocuted, and her mind had gone completely blank. She hadn't been able to move, hadn't been able to say anything. That was probably because the car had hit her so abruptly that she'd never had a chance to think before…

Feeling the vibrations coming from the phone on her chest, Emily gazed at it, pulling the device from the charger and staring at the screen. She'd woken up at the same time as her vibrating alarm had begun to buzz. Maybe if the alarm hadn't been there to wake her, her brain would have shown her something past dying, fabricated something else for her to experience? Or maybe she would have woken up regardless.

Emily silenced the alarm and clambered from her tiny bed, her heart still beating quickly. She placed a hand over her heart and realised that she could feel it slamming against her ribs like a prisoner trying to break free of their cell, like a drummer finishing a climactic song.

After sliding to her feet, Emily stood, quickly climbed into her work clothes and walked towards her mirror, gazing at herself. Her long, light blonde hair was as tangled as usual.

Emily dropped into the seat in front of her make-up table and grabbed her hairbrush, painfully brushing the knots out of her locks before, once she'd placed the hairbrush back onto the surface, she examined her face. A small spot was beginning to form on her left cheek, a little bump interrupting the regular smoothness of her pale skin.

After quickly applying a small amount of concealer to the area, effectively hiding the spot, Emily paused. She'd done that in her dream. The spot had been in the exact same place. How had she known that one was going to form there?

Emily shrugged the thought from her mind, chalking it up to a strange coincidence. Maybe she'd scratched her face while she'd been asleep, had felt the beginning of the spot and had pictured it in her dream. That was probably what had happened.

Emily then stood, heading towards the kitchen after having grabbed her phone, wanting breakfast.

It took a few minutes for Emily to make her toast, having spread a small amount of butter onto the bread before she flopped onto the couch, the plate resting on the space in front of her, her feet pressing against the arm of the seat at the other end as she propped herself up. One hand held the TV remote as she flicked through the free channels, searching for something to watch.

After Emily had stopped on a channel, she noticed that the content which was playing was the same as what had played in her dream. She couldn't remember the exact details of what she'd previously seen, but there was a similar premise, at least, something which Emily pondered slightly but shrugged off. She'd probably seen the low-budget show at some point before. Maybe she was watching a re-run. Maybe she'd seen the episode before and had recalled it in her dream, it simply being a coincidence that the same episode was playing on the screen in front of her.

Emily finished her breakfast, remained in front of the TV for a while and, after checking the time, saw that it was time to leave.

After standing up and placing her plate in the sink and brushing her teeth over the bathroom sink, Emily walked to her room, grabbed her coat, then walked out of her apartment, checking to make sure that she had everything while walking away from her newly locked door. Phone, money, keys. She had everything which she would need.

After descending the stairs and making her way out of the door, Emily felt the light, cool breeze on her face and realised that it was a good idea to have decided to wear a coat, especially as the sky was slightly grey and it looked as if it was going to rain at some point.

Emily began the journey, seeing immediately that the traffic was as bad as usual. Given that it was nearing nine in the morning, Emily knew that plenty of people were on their way to work or school, making the roads and the pavement fairly busy. It definitely didn't help that Emily lived in a city, either.

And so began Emily's stop-and-start journey, having to pause at almost each road which cut across the pavement, at least two cars using the passage, making Emily and the surrounding people halt their journey to allow for the vehicles to pass. Such a thing occurred a few times, gradually making Emily more and more frustrated as she would usually become, not liking the inconvenience.

It didn't take too long for the roof of the shop which Emily worked in to become visible. Emily stood about two-hundred metres away, waiting for three cars to move so that she could cross to the continuation of the pavement on the other side. As soon as Emily saw the roof, she gave a light smile, definitely preferring the idea of being at work than the idea of travelling through the slow hellhole which was the streets leading to the shop.

After another few minutes, Emily made her way across the car park and into the store, immediately heading to the break room so that she could clock-in. She b-lined straight to the door to the back room, not saying anything to the two colleagues whom she passed as she made her way, pushing through the doors to the back room before making her way towards the door to the break room.

Emily drew a small tick beside her name before she placed the pen back into the holder, took a step back and let out a small sigh. She was finding it slightly odd that what she was experiencing was the same as what she'd experienced in her dream, but she could only guess that it was the case as every day was a meticulous routine. If she was in work, she'd do the exact same thing, more or less. The only changes would come when she'd have a day off, though she mostly spent that time doing one of two things: relaxing at home or spending time with a few friends. Emily guessed that her dream had simply copied her regular life to each, exact detail.

Emily began the day slowly, dealing with a few basic chores. She began replacing any items which needed to be replaced, aiding the occasional customer, helping out in the check-out area until, about an hour into her shift, the first rush-hour began, cementing Emily to the till as she dealt with customer after customer.

"Have a nice day," Emily stated with a monotone voice and a forced smile to a young girl who was very clearly skipping school, not appearing to be ill and definitely not looking old enough to be considered a graduate.

After gazing down the conveyor belt, Emily saw that there were only two more customers to deal with before she could leave the last few to whoever was controlling the other till.

As soon as Emily had finished with the second customer, she closed the till and went straight to the break room, thinking that she deserved a break for having worked for over an hour straight.

After entering the break room, Emily saw that a few others had the same idea, taking small breaks. The break room wasn't very big, so relaxing wasn't very easy. Emily even gave up on leaning back and taking a breather, spending the fifteen-minute-long break which she was taking on her phone, scrolling through social media to pass the time and tapping her foot to the beat of a song which was stuck in her head.

It was only when two more employees entered the break room and another two left that Emily decided to get back to work, following the two employees from the room and back to the main area of the shop.

Lunch came and went in a flash, Emily not seeing the time approaching as she was busy getting on with work. When the inevitable rush-hour arrived, she helped out on a till, making a little, polite conversation with a few customers, including an older gentleman whom she could have sworn had tried to look the neck of her shirt, making her recoil, realising that the same thing had happened in her dream… and that the guy in her dream looked identical to the man who was stood in front of her.

"You can keep the change," the man grumbled, giving a strange, toothy smile before he took his receipt from Emily, making sure to brush her fingers lightly with his, all the while Emily staring at him, bewildered. As soon as the man had left, Emily stared into thin air for a moment until another customer snapped her out of her stupor. She shook the moment off until things quieted down before retreating to the break room for half-an-hour to eat lunch and to have a small rest, trying not to ponder the occurrence too much.

From her lunch break to back to work, Emily found herself engrossed in her job except for when the distracting thought of the older man would pop into her head and confuse her. She'd been thinking that the whole day had been the same as her dream as each day would usually follow the same events, but for such a thing to be identical to how it had been in her dream? And something so… unpredictable, too? Emily felt extremely odd thinking about that. She felt like she was reliving the exact same day and, in a sense, she was. The only difference seemed to be that she was conscious of the oddity of the situation and that…

She was going to die. She'd been struck by a car in her dream and had died. If everything which had happened in her dream was happening and was going to happen in real life, then she was destined to die, right?

Emily leaned her back into the shelf which she'd

just finished stacking, feeling the structure of it wobble slightly due to the force, a single can of green beans tumbling and smacking into the floor with a clang. She moved forwards and scooped it up, quickly returning it the shelf, trying to shake the thought from her head. All which she had to do was avoid the car, right? It wasn't like she was *destined* to die. She could avoid it. Maybe the dream had been like some type of warning, something to tell her to avoid that car. Maybe that was it. Maybe that was why the death had felt so strangely real to her.

All which she had to do was avoid dying. But, Emily realised, petrified, what if she couldn't change the event? What if she could avoid the car but would be killed by another? What if she would be extremely careful when crossing the road only for a vehicle to swerve from the road and slam into her? She'd still die. She wouldn't escape the fate. What if she couldn't prevent her death? What if she couldn't change *anything*?

Emily ran down the aisle, disregarding the box filled with products which were supposed to refill the shelves. She ignored the gazes of confused customers and the cut-off question of the employee whom she zoomed past. She was going to keep working at the till. That was what she was going to do. She'd spent this time in her dream working in the aisles, not scanning items and sending people on their way. If she could work on a till, it would be different, and maybe that would prove to her that she could save her life. Maybe she could survive.

As soon as Emily had arrived in the till area, she lightly shoehorned the employee who was already there away, assuring her that she could take over as if she was doing it out of the kindness of her heart, like working at the till was some type of torture.

It took a moment for the customers to disappear, all of them having been served, but as soon as they'd left, Emily took over, dropping into the seat and closing the gate-counter, letting out a light sigh. There was already a difference. If there was going to be something to say that she couldn't work at the till, something which would force her back to the aisles to work there, then at least she'd already made a slight change by being in charge of the main till for a period.

After a small amount of time, a customer placed a few items onto the conveyor belt, properly beginning Emily's act of defiance against what she guessed was laid out for her.

A few hours passed, Emily spending as much time as possible working at the check-out. She was pulled away two hours in, though, another employee insisting for her to have a break given that she'd served what must have been close to one-hundred people, so she agreed, tired and sure that the change was big enough to prevent her death from happening. She didn't even know if her idea was going to work, but what did she have to lose? Without doing anything differently, she'd probably die, and it would be for real this time! Emily was petrified of the idea of death. She'd already technically experienced it once, and she wasn't a fan of the feeling.

After Emily's thirty-minute break, she returned to stacking shelves and helping the occasional customer to find something, eventually making it to the end of her workday where she grabbed her coat and waited for five minutes to leave. She hoped that she would be able to avoid the car which possibly had her name on the bonnet, but she realised after a small amount of waiting that she would still be in the cataclysm of traffic, so she decided to just go home.

After crossing the car park and then extremely cautiously crossing the road, her head going from left to right every second, scared of a car somehow sneaking up on her, she made it to the other side of the street.

Emily breathed a sigh of relief when she made it to the other side of the road. She was unharmed. She only had to walk for another fifteen minutes to get back to her apartment, then she would be safe, right?

And so began Emily's cautious, paranoid trip home, walking slower than usual, making sure to stay as far away from the side of the road as possible, not wanting there to be a chance of another pedestrian knocking into her and sending her flying onto the tarmac, a vehicle angled perfectly to crush her skull like what had happened in her dream.

Whenever Emily would have to cross over a small stretch of a street, she would pause and stare in both directions which any vehicles could come from. She'd look both ways what would be at least six times each before she'd begin to cross, hurrying constantly, not wanting to spend too much time while being stood on the tarmac. She sprinted once, knowing that the road was busy, feeling that she'd be hit if she would walk.

Emily continued her actions, making her way home gradually, until she came to the crossing where she'd died in her dream. She stared both ways, petrified. She could feel herself sweating, something which had gradually built-up over the course of her journey, but she was aware of it now. She could tell that her back was damp, was fairly certain that the work shirt which she wore underneath her coat was a different colour. It didn't matter that it was a slightly chilly day, she was sweating regardless just due to the paranoia and the fear which she felt building over every passing second.

Emily stepped onto the road slowly, cautiously, then broke-out into a hasty sprint, making it to the other side of the road within seconds.

A few people surrounding Emily looked at her, some looking bewildered or confused while others looked slightly entertained at the prospect of a grown woman being petrified of crossing the road, but they didn't know what was rushing around Emily's mind, piercing each thought with the reminder that she could die within any moment.

After making it across the road, Emily simply continued her antics until she entered her apartment building. She began to ascend the stairs, wanting to flop onto her couch and to cry from the built-up stress and fear which she could still feel even though she'd passed the point where she'd previously been killed.

Maybe it was just a weird coincidence, Emily wondered as she approached her door, pulling her keys from her pocket. *Maybe I've seen that man somewhere before...*

Emily stepped into her apartment, closed the door and pulled her coat off extremely quickly, letting out a long sigh before she chucked the jacket onto the floor. She didn't care that it was slobby to throw it on the floor, too hot to bear wearing it for any longer and too tired to face carrying it to her bedroom so that she could hang it up. The stress, the fear, the way-too-loud thoughts had made her exhausted. She felt as if she'd just ran three marathons in a row. Her legs felt as if their bones were melting, something which she knew was being caused by her anxiety. She needed to sit down, she needed to clean the sweat from her body... she needed a bath.

After confirming with herself that she could be bothered to bathe and not drop into bed five or six hours earlier than usual, Emily staggered towards the bathroom, pushing the door open and immediately turning both taps on, not caring about the temperature of the water, only wanting the tub to fill-up.

Emily stripped, pulling all of her clothes off and disregarding them on the floor before she sat on the edge of the bath, watching as the water filled the tub. She urged it to go faster, the water only filling about a third of the amount which she wanted. She just craved the ability to sink into the water and to let her muscles loosen. She needed a decent thirty minutes to sit and ponder.

It took another few minutes for the bath to fill, the water ending up at a fairly decent temperature. It wasn't too hot and it wasn't too cold, so Emily didn't find it hard to let herself slide into the tub, a small amount of water splashing over the side and landing on the bathmat.

She immediately closed her eyes, leaning back. It was lucky that she was short enough to be able to stretch-out fully, her feet extremely close to being pressed against the plastic underneath the two taps. She could relax properly, close her eyes and just try to think about whatever she wanted to think about.

Emily tried to consider the dream, tried to consider the parallels between it and reality, but stopped herself once she found herself trying to figure out just what it meant. She could figure that out later. She was probably too tired to come up with something which would make sense, anyway. All which she could come up with while laying in the bath, her arms resting on top of the water, was the thought that she was psychic, something which she didn't entirely rule out as she quite liked the idea of being a one-of-a-kind type of person, but knew that there was probably a much more realistic explanation.

As soon as Emily had decided to let the thoughts wait until the next day, she felt herself sliding further down the side of the tub, her knees bending to ensure that she had enough space to do so. Her shoulders were starting to get cold, so she wanted to keep them warm underneath the water. Not to mention that it was beginning to get cosier and cosier…

Before she really knew what was happening, Emily began to fall asleep. Her eyelids drooped, her head lolled towards her left shoulder, then her breathing steadied and her heartrate slowed.

Then she fell asleep, unaware as the muscles in her knees which were keeping her in position relaxed, allowing for her to slide deeper and deeper into the bathtub.

Emily's instinct kicked in, but she didn't wake up. She didn't slosh around. Instead, she held her breath until she had to let it out and replace it, inhaling water, filling her lungs with the slightly dirty bathwater.

Yet, still, Emily didn't wake up.

Chapter 3

Emily jolted awake as she had the day before, ripping her sleeping mask from her head alongside her earmuffs, staring at the ceiling.

She'd drowned.

She'd been dreaming again.

Both facts hit her at once, the two of them fighting for dominance, both of them wanting to be the thing to overwhelm her, creating a messy, swirling cacophony of fear and confusion.

It took a moment for Emily to decide to move, sliding out of her bed, her vibrating, charging phone sliding off of her chest, thumping on the bed, making her jump. She felt extremely on edge. Her head felt slightly light and she wasn't certain that her lungs were clear of water.

What was going on?

Emily unplugged her phone and turned the vibrating alarm off, taking a moment to breathe before she pulled her work clothes on and looked in the mirror. Her hair was tangled as it always was.

After dropping into the seat by her make-up table, Emily paused for a moment, her eyes closed as she psyched herself to look at her left cheek. As soon as she'd opened her eyes, her gaze drifting towards the reflection of her left cheek in the mirror, she spotted the light bump and threw herself backwards, jumping out of the seat and backing towards the wall by her tall mirror.

"What's going on?" She almost whimpered to herself, looking around the room frantically as if searching for something which was causing the oddity of her situation. The spot was there. It was in the same place. Was she still dreaming? Was she going to die again?

Emily paused for a moment. She knew about lucid dreams. If she *was* asleep, she would be able to control the dream, right? She'd be able to do whatever she'd like, would be able to force herself to wake up, right?

Emily stared at her make-up table. *Float* she urged, not knowing what else to urge for. *Float. Float. Float!* "Float!" Emily let out, practically shouting the word.

The table didn't move.

After a moment of feeling like an idiot, Emily let out a somewhat relieved sigh. She wasn't asleep, then, right? If she couldn't force something to happen, she wasn't asleep.

Emily slid back into the seat in front of the make-up table. "Third time's the charm, I guess," she mumbled to herself.

After applying the small amount of concealer and tackling the knots in her hair, Emily left the room, snatching her phone from her bed and heading into the kitchen to make herself some toast.

Emily made her breakfast, dropped onto the couch and began to flick through the various TV channels. She landed on the same low-budget show which she'd watched twice. What was happening in the show was the same as what she'd seen twice before, something which didn't give Emily much hope. As she saw it, it didn't matter very much if she would be living the same day again. After all, she'd avoided being hit by that car and had drowned instead, so it was possible to change things and have different outcomes. All which she would have to do would be to find the correct formula for survival.

As she had previously, Emily wasted time until she needed to leave, placing her crumb-covered plate into the sink, brushing her teeth, grabbing her coat, then checking to make sure that she had her phone, money and keys before she left.

After stepping onto the street, feeling the same slightly chilly breeze which she'd grown accustomed to, Emily began walking. She tried not to think about the oddity of her situation. It was hard to comprehend, after all. She was living through the same day again and again, she'd already died twice and had woken up at the beginning of the day as if the occurrence had been a dream. She still wasn't entirely certain that she wasn't *still* asleep, only using the fact that she hadn't turned the nightmare into a lucid dream or into a lucid nightmare as proof that she was, finally, awake. Or, at the very least, she supposed, if she *wasn't* awake, she'd found that she had no way of forcing herself to wake up or of forcing other things to happen. She could only control herself as she could in real life.

What do I change now? Emily asked herself as she dodged a schoolgirl who hurried down the street, possibly late for something. *I tried to alter my workday and I stayed at the shop for a bit. I didn't get killed by that car, so maybe…*

Emily continued to ponder, unable to come up with a stable plan until she realised that she was nearing the shop.

I'll make even more changes to my workday, she concluded quickly, not wanting to get to work before coming up with a plan. She guessed that changing something else about her workday could possibly prevent her from drowning. Maybe taking it a little easier so that she wouldn't be worn down? But how would she take it easier?

Emily walked into the shop and glanced in the direction of the check-outs. *That's it*! She thought, smiling to herself. She'd spend as much time as possible working at a till. She'd be sitting down, and she'd only be scanning items and talking to the people who would spark conversations. She knew that she wouldn't be able to stay there for the entire day, but she could at least spend as much time there as possible. That would be different from spending the majority of the day stacking shelves, plus she could be much more sociable, something which would be another change.

I'll be less tired, more sociable and doing a

different task for most of the day, Emily summarised in her head. *If that doesn't change anything, what will?*

Emily walked into the back room, headed to the break room, clocked-in and then immediately started to head to the check-out area. She insisted that she would work there, telling the woman who'd been there previously to have a break, that she was always working at the till. It was a shot in the dark as Emily didn't know if the statement was true, but the woman seemed to accept it, giving Emily the position before wandering off in search of a task.

The day kicked off slowly. Emily chatted politely to the occasional customer who would begin to say something, tried to make herself sound enthusiastic and happy to be there, hiding her worry that she was going to face another death later in the day.

It was only when the first rush-hour hit that the older gentlemen whom she'd seen previously entered the shop, Emily able to see him from a dozen metres away. Why was he early? Had he originally been in the shop twice, or had that changed?

By the time that the man arrived at the check-out, nothing more than a bottle of water in his hand, he stood in front of Emily, staring at her, waiting for the bottle to slowly slide towards her as it rested on the conveyor belt.

Emily tried to avoid eye-contact with the man, feeling uncomfortable. She didn't know if he was doing something in the moment which made her feel odd, but her previous experiences with him were on her mind.

He'd almost definitely been trying to look down the neck of her shirt, and she could have sworn that he'd deliberately brushed her fingers with his while taking his receipt before. What would he try this time?

"Having a good day?" Emily questioned as she swiped the bottle from the conveyor belt as soon as it was within reach, quickly scanning it and placing it in front of the man.

"I suppose," the man replied, his voice slightly gruff. He pulled out more money than what was necessary to pay for the cheap bottle of water, hesitating for a moment before grabbing Emily's hand, taking it from its resting place on the counter and prying her fist open.

Emily watched, about to say something before she felt the money in her hand. The man closed her fist around it. "Keep that money," he said, grinning a little, his brown eyes slightly narrowed as if trying to intimidate her which, whether it was the intention or not, he was succeeding with.

Emily stared at the money in her hand. It wasn't a luxurious amount, but it was definitely way more than the usual waiter would receive as a tip for their service. It almost felt…

"Inappropriate," Emily let out accidentally, though she played along with it as if she'd intended to speak. She slid the money towards the man. "I can't keep this."

The man stared at her, looking almost bewildered. "What?" He let out, possibly confused and slightly annoyed.

Emily took the money which was needed for the payment, placed it into the cash register and printed the man's receipt, sliding it towards him, knowing that he couldn't possibly be creepy while picking it up.

The man paused, took the receipt, the money and his bottle of water, then walked out of the shop without a word.

Emily felt stupid then. The man had been annoying her and creeping her out, but it probably wasn't the best thing to anger him and to gain a slight enemy when she was trying to stop herself from being killed by various things.

Emily continued with her shift, remaining at the check-out for a small while until another employee insisted for her to have a break, prompting her to go to the break room and to have lunch early, feeling satisfied as she knew that she'd changed the day a decent amount. Maybe angering that creepy man had been a good idea as it had been something completely new. Maybe that was somehow the key to being able to avoid another death- provided that she was going to have to face another, of course.

After Emily had finished her lunch, she returned to work, stacking shelves and helping customers for a while before she had to help out in the check-out area due to the rush-hour. While there, scanning some items, wishing people a good day, Emily noticed something in her peripheral vision. The man was back, waiting to be served as he had both times before. Emily wondered if the interaction was going to go unchanged regardless of the fact that they'd interacted earlier in the day, but she doubted that such a thing would be the case. Maybe it would be a good idea to have another employee watching the situation…

The man stepped to the front of the till, stood in front of Emily. "Are you going to accept my money this time?" He asked quietly, Emily barely hearing the question over the beep of his purchase being scanned.

"What?" Emily let out, placing the packaged sandwich in front of him. "Oh- no," she answered, shaking her head quickly. "As I said, it's inappropriate."

The man grumbled something which Emily didn't hear before paying and leaving immediately, not bothering with the receipt or even for Emily to give him his change. She didn't want to keep it, guessing that he'd wanted to leave her with the spare money so that she'd pocket it, and so she placed it into the cash register, not knowing what else to do.

The rest of her shift passed fairly quickly and uneventfully. Emily was shoehorned away from the till again after another thirty-minutes of working there, and so spent the remainder of her shift stocking shelves and walking around slightly aimlessly.

When it was time to leave, Emily decided to leave straight away, and quickly, too, wanting to hopefully make a decent amount of the journey home before the worst of the traffic would pile-up. She was going to keep an eye out for cars, something which she knew for a fact wasn't going to slip her mind easily, and she wasn't going to have a bath upon getting home. Instead, she was going to order a take-out, slightly scared of cooking, and would eat it in front of the TV before having an early night. To Emily, that sounded fairly safe, so she didn't expect that anything bad would happen.

After leaving the shop and crossing the road, Emily realised that the street was much quieter than she was initially expecting, though she could tell that chaos was about to ensue, prompting her to hurry slightly, not wanting to get caught in a mob of pedestrians.

As she hurried home, Emily thought, wondering what would happen the next day- if she would make it to the next day- as she didn't know if her situation was just going to continue or if she was in some type of strange loop as if living in a short video game, playing the same level over and over again. Emily was so preoccupied with her thoughts that she didn't notice the man stepping out in front of her.

"Down that alleyway," the creepy man let out, almost snarling.

Emily stopped in her tracks, staring at the old man, scared.

"Are you... stalking me?" She questioned, but quickly silenced herself when she noticed what was in the man's left hand: a gun held to be level with his hip, tilted to point at her chest.

"*Down the alleyway,*" he repeated, his voice sounding strained as he forced it through his teeth. He took a step towards Emily, motioning with a sideways nod towards the alleyway in question.

"What are you..." Emily began, millions of situations flying through her mind, though she was unable to focus on one possible outcome at a time. Was he going to mug her? Kidnap her? Rape her? Murder her?

Emily followed the man's orders, not knowing what else to do, petrified due to the pistol pointing at her. She walked into the alleyway slowly, extremely carefully, treading lightly as if scared that making a noise would cause the gun to fire automatically.

After making it halfway down the alleyway, the man behind her told her to turn around. Emily stopped and turned around slowly, holding her hands up as if trying to prove that she didn't have a weapon on her. "What do you want?" She asked, her voice shaking. She could feel that she wanted to cry, her bottom lip quivering slightly, the corners of her eyes burning.

The man took a small step closer. "You were rude to me," he grunted, pulling the gun up to point it directly at Emily's head. "I did a kind thing, and you rejected me."

"Well, I'm sorry, *sir*, but it isn't the twenties anymore," Emily let out shakily before she could stop herself, deciding to follow-up on the quip, wanting to seem fearless. "You can't buy a woman."

The man tilted his head to the left slightly and cocked a white eyebrow. "But I *can* kill the ones who don't comply."

Emily rushed forwards, slamming into the man,

pushing him over and into the wall before she sprinted towards the opening of the alleyway. The man was elderly, probably in his late sixties of early seventies. He wouldn't be able to keep up with her, right?

But Emily forgot that a bullet could.

Chapter 4

Emily threw herself forwards, the momentum from her dream somehow carrying into consciousness as she flew towards the end of her bed, her phone flying from her chest and clattering to the ground, still plugged into her charger.

Emily rested at the end of the bed, her head hanging off the end of it as she panted before pulling the sleeping mask and the earmuffs from her head. She'd been shot that time, right through the heart and then through the head. It had been a quick death, but that didn't make it any more pleasant than drowning or being struck by a car.

After a moment of laying there, breathing heavily, her heart still pounding from the experience, Emily slid from her bed, shakily getting to her feet. She went to pull her work clothes on, though stopped herself. There was a pattern. All three times which she'd died previously had been related to work, right? She'd been hit by a car on her way home from work, she'd ended up drowning due to passing out because of the stress which came from being hit by that car, and she'd been shot because of the creepy man whom she'd met at work. What would happen if she would stay at home?

Emily stood up straight and looked at herself in the mirror as she thought about the possibility. Would it change much? Yes, obviously, so it would lead to a different outcome. Plus, she'd be much safer at home. She could sit on the couch and watch TV all day. Where would the danger be? Becoming so relaxed that her heart would stop beating?

Emily jumped for her phone, swiping it up from the floor before she unlocked it and went to her contacts, looking for her manager's number. She was nice, so Emily didn't doubt that she'd be allowed to have the day off, especially because she hadn't taken a day off in what must have been at least three months, so one sick day would be allowed, surely.

After dialling the manager's number, Emily held the phone to her ear and closed her eyes, trying to think of how someone with a cold would sound.

"Hello?" Came from the phone, startling Emily slightly even though she'd been expecting the voice.

"Hello," Emily rasped, cringing slightly as she feared that she was overdoing it. "I'm ill."

There was silence on the other end. "Okay, Emily," her manager replied slowly, her voice soft and slightly soothing. "How long do you think you'll need off?"

Emily paused, surprised. That had been much easier than she'd expected initially. "Just day, probably," she replied. "It's just a sore throat and some sniffling," she explained, quickly faking a sniffle to prove her point.

"Okay," her manager replied. "I'll have someone cover for you if they can. Make sure to relax, okay?"

"I know," Emily replied, chuckling slightly. She'd been slightly fearing that the approach wouldn't work, that her manager would see right through her fake cold and would instruct her to go into work anyway, but the whole thing had been entirely smooth, not to mention quick, no bumps or creases to be seen.

The call ended, prompting Emily to flop back onto her bed, crawling underneath the covers, pulling them around herself tightly. She'd be safe in bed, definitely. The only danger would be suffocating herself on her pillow, but she didn't think that such a thing would happen, mainly because she wasn't expecting to get to sleep for very long. She just wanted a small lie-in.

After sliding her phone onto the bedside table, Emily's mind began to drift to the situation. What was going on? Why was she being tormented with death after death, and why was she waking up afterwards as if the whole thing had been a dream? Had the last time *really* been a dream, she would have been able to have made it into a lucid dream, so, if it really *was* a dream, why had such an approach failed? And if it wasn't a dream, what *was* it?

"This is a mess," Emily mumbled to herself as she closed her eyes, her head sinking into the comfort of her recently washed pillow. The whole situation felt like something more than what it was. Even though Emily saw it as some type of game, the objective being to survive the whole day, she felt as if it was something more, some type of test, for instance, maybe a sick trick played by a demon, or whatever. Whatever was *really* going on felt unhinged and too complicated for Emily to understand, let alone think of.

It didn't take very long for Emily to drift to sleep, all questioning thoughts about the situation fading from her mind like a headache being cured by rest. It was only when Emily woke up at ten that she was reminded of the situation, a strange wonder passing through her mind.

What happens now that I've slept again? She wondered, sliding out of bed, wanting breakfast. It was a valid question. After every death, she'd woken up at the same time and in the same place. Now that she'd been asleep again, had she created a new checkpoint? Was she going to wake up at ten if she'd die again, or would she go back to waking up at the same time as before?

Emily quickly concluded that there were a lot of things regarding her situation which weren't going to be answered without testing. She would have to die and wake up again to see when she'd awaken. She would have to live through her workday while altering tiny aspects to see if she could live through the entire day. She would have to figure out how big of change would be needed to result in a different outcome, whether positive or negative.

As soon as the toast had popped out of her

toaster, Emily spread some butter onto it and dropped it onto her plate, moving to the couch to browse through the TV channels.

Emily spent a small amount of time eating, at one point ending up having a coughing fit as a crumb went down her windpipe, scaring her immensely as she thought that she was going to die, but she managed to get it out and avoid another death. After having disposed of the plate in the sink and brushed her teeth in the bathroom, Emily simply returned to the couch, continuing to watch the low-budget show, at a point where she was watching parts which she hadn't seen before.

When lunch arrived, Emily ate in front of the TV, beginning to feel lazy and having to convince herself that she wasn't being lazy by staying safe and preventing her death.

With each bite of her sandwich, Emily found her thoughts drifting towards the situation. She couldn't help it. She wanted to distract herself from what was going on, but somehow couldn't. It was like her focus was attached to a rope which was being pulled, shifting her attention's gaze to the death-loop instead of what she was watching or, unfortunately, each mouthful.

Emily began to choke. She knew immediately that she'd taken a larger-than-average bite and that she hadn't chewed it enough. She could feel that half of it was stuck in her windpipe and that half of it was stuck in her oesophagus.

Emily grasped at her throat out of instinct,

accidentally knocking the plate to the floor where it smashed. She rolled off of the couch, hoping that the impact of landing would dislodge the food, but she landed on a shard of the plate and felt her spine jolt from the jagged edge of it.

Rolling around, trying to figure out what to do, Emily's eyes darted around the room in search of something which could aid her to get the food out, but she couldn't find anything except for the coffee table just in front of her...

Emily threw herself at the coffee table, angling herself so that her back would hit the edge of it, but nothing happened. She fell to the floor and cut the inside of her forearm on a piece of the broken plate.

Emily could feel tears coming from her eyes, either because of the pain and the discomfiture which she was experiencing or because she was running out of oxygen. Moving around so much hadn't been a good idea. She'd used most of her oxygen up within a few movements.

She resorted to trying to cough. Nothing. Then tried to swallow. Nothing. Emily could feel her consciousness beginning to slip, but she forced herself to stay awake, straining the muscles in her eyelids. Though, even though her eyes were open, black spots were beginning to obscure her vision.

Come on! She urged mentally, using her hands to try to push at her throat, hoping that she could remove the food like that.

All which Emily ended up doing was scratching

her neck, only amplifying the pain. She rolled onto her back and threw herself into the air as best as possible, slamming the top of her back into the ground. Nothing.

Emily passed out.

Chapter 5

Yet again, as expected, Emily jolted awake and pulled her sleeping mask and earmuffs from her head, looking around the room, wondering what time it was. Was there a chance that she'd woken up at ten this time?

Emily's phone vibrated on her chest, something which she noticed quickly. It was the normal time. Sleeping and waking up again hadn't made any difference whatsoever.

After sliding out of bed, Emily stood and began to pull her work clothes on instinctively, pausing for a moment to debate inwardly whether or not to try staying home again, but she guessed that she'd just end up dying from something else unexpected. She'd began chocking and hadn't been able to dislodge the food despite her frenzied attempts. She was probably doomed to death in similar ways no matter what she would do while staying at home because there wasn't much to change, and she didn't really want to separate herself from all food suddenly. Maybe the death was some type of punishment for taking an easier route?

As Emily pulled her clothes on, she wondered if there was something specific which she was supposed to do. Maybe she was supposed to live through a perfect day. Maybe she would have to make the day completely average. There was definitely a chance that she wouldn't be able to figure out what to do, that she'd keep dying over and over in an endless loop.

Emily didn't bother to look in the mirror, simply dropped into the seat by her make-up table and began to brush her hair. She didn't bother to apply concealer, not caring at this point. Any impression which she'd make on people would undoubtedly be useless as she'd most likely end up dead.

No, Emily told herself. *Don't think like that.*

She walked into the kitchen, grabbing her phone from her bed on her way out, and quickly made breakfast, slightly hesitant to eat due to the fact that she'd died from asphyxiation, but knowing that she probably wouldn't have to suffer that fate again given that she was returning to work.

Emily ate, watched the TV and brushed her teeth before leaving the apartment, descending the stairs and stepping onto the street. The process of just getting on with her boring, identical day was beginning to feel like some type of routine, something which startled Emily slightly when she noticed it, though she quickly brushed it off. She was adapting to her situation, and that was good, right? She would be calmer and, therefore, she'd think more rationally about every choice, something which would probably increase her chances of survival much more than if she would rush around, terrified and confused.

The journey began, Emily weaving around the

steadily increasing number of pedestrians as the vehicles began to pile-up on the road.

It took a small amount of time- maybe not that much longer than ten minutes- for Emily to see the shop in the distance. The pavement had become crowded very suddenly, and the road was just as full as it had been on previous days.

What am I going to change this time? Emily questioned, realising that she didn't really have a plan. She'd tried spending more time in the check-out area and had been much more sociable, but neither attempts had given any promising results. What else was there to do?

Emily tried to think as she closed the distance between her and the shop, coming up with something as she walked through the doors: she would be as antisocial as possible. Even though she'd usually spend her workday avoiding a decent amount of contact, she would still do her job, she'd still help customers whenever they would ask her for help, she'd occasionally make small talk with co-workers whenever she would get bored, so speaking to *no-one* at all would be a change; it was something to try, at least.

Emily walked to the break room, clocking-in before getting to work, grabbing a box of products from the back before taking them to the main area, beginning to replace items with new ones.

The day dragged on, Emily not socialising at all. Whenever a customer would come up to her, she would either redirect them to another co-worker, muttering that she couldn't help them, or she'd avoid customers altogether. She'd see someone looking confused, clearly looking for something, and would turn around and walk in the opposite direction, essentially running away from her duty. She felt bad for doing it, but she was adamant that she would commit to the plan entirely. She wanted to make sure that she was consistent, scared that nothing would change otherwise and that she would end up being hit by a car on her way home given that the day would end up being so similar to the first day which she'd experienced of this nightmare.

It was only when the first rush-hour came that Emily's co-workers took notice of her anti-social behaviour, unable to say anything due to being so busy, though two of them made an effort to corner her in the break room afterwards.

"How come you're not talking to anyone?" One of them, a middle-aged man whom Emily barely new asked her, his tone of voice sounding slightly accusing but also slightly concerned. To Emily, it sounded as if he wanted to be angry with her but was worried that something was wrong.

"Yeah, you haven't worked at the check-out at all! You barely helped with that rush-hour!" Another young girl, someone slightly younger than Emily who had started only a few months before, demanded, not making any effort to conceal her annoyance.

Emily remained quiet, debating what to do. She didn't want to ignore them and just walk out of the break room. Even though she wanted to commit to being antisocial, the cornering was something new, so she'd already made a change.

"I'm just... tired," Emily replied meekly, hoping that her answer wouldn't infuriate them.

"Tired?" The man repeated, looking surprised. "That's it? You just haven't had a coffee yet?"

"I don't drink coffee," Emily stated, her voice even but still quiet, feeling stupid. She could sense that some type of argument was approaching, and she wanted to avoid it as much as possible.

"Then go to bed earlier," the girl commanded, her voice sharp, illustrating her feelings extremely well. She paused for a moment, then stood up and stormed out of the break room, probably trying to avoid lashing out too much at Emily and causing a scene. She hadn't even been in the break room for very long, maybe only having spent a few minutes in there.

Emily remained silent as she stared at her phone, scrolling through social media, ignoring the man who continued to look at her. His face was relaxed, he looked calm, meaning that Emily couldn't tell if he was annoyed with her or not. She didn't even know if he was planning on saying anything else, watching her silently.

"Is something else wrong?" The man asked her extremely quietly, almost as if he was scared of being overheard despite there being no-one else in the room with them.

"No," Emily whispered back, accidentally sarcastic, her tone with a tinge of mockery, something which the man clearly didn't appreciate as he leaned back in his chair, looking hesitant about something before he stood up and walked out the room, following the young girl. Emily heard him mutter something on his way out, distinctly hearing something about her being a bitch before the door closed.

Emily let out a long and deep sigh, closing her eyes and letting her head loll forwards slightly. She felt terrible for being so... moody? Distant? However she was acting, she felt terrible for doing so.

Emily's break lasting for a few more minutes before she decided to get back to work, remaining in the backroom, knowing that she needed to get a box from one of the shelves.

The way which she was acting and upsetting her co-workers was playing on her mind. Even though she usually wasn't extremely sociable, she wasn't mean by any regard, so ignoring people and redirecting them, saying selfish things... stuff like that just didn't sit right in Emily's mind, whether someone else was doing it or, in this case, because *she* was doing it.

Emily continued to think, trying to forget about the trouble which she was causing her co-workers as she removed a box from a shelf with a forklift, slowly lowering it to the ground, slightly scared that she'd fumble it and drop it given that she was distracted, though, thankfully, no such thing happened.

Emily hopped out of the forklift, moving to grab the handle of the trolley which she'd placed the box onto, though she paused and, after a moment, began to lean against the shelves, rubbing at her eyes slightly.

She was still stressed about everything and, as a result, mentally drained. Would it be good to play into the mean-girl attitude a little more and have some extra time off to regain some energy?

After considering it for a moment, the idea of a nap came into Emily's mind and, upon thinking about how much she'd appreciate being able to have a nap, she felt a yawn building.

Emily let the yawn out, stretching her arms out slightly as she did so as if she'd just woken up, her left arm knocking into a box, making her jump a little, the impact having been unexpected.

Emily quickly turned to look at the shelves, scared that something would fall off even though she'd barely applied enough force to knock anything over. Nothing happened.

With a relieved sigh, Emily clambered back into the forklift to return it to its original position. But she forgot to switch it to reverse.

As soon as Emily had pressed on the accelerator, she realised her mistake, though it was too late, the forklift moved forwards, a beam stabbing through a box, pushing it backwards slightly. It didn't fall off of the edge, speared by the beam as it leaned into the shelves...

The gigantic storage shelf began to tilt, Emily paralysed with fear. What could she do? If she'd reverse, she'd pull the box into the shelves and pull them over, but she couldn't move forwards, either, as the forklift would push the shelves over. They wouldn't land on her, but it would end with her getting fired, and if she *didn't* die afterwards, would her reality return to normal with her unemployed?

Emily tried to scoot from the seat of the forklift, sliding out slowly until she was stood on the ground. She'd pull the box from the beam, then she'd reverse the forklift away from the shelves. That's how she'd deal with the situation.

Instinctively, Emily looked up. The shelf was tilting towards her ever so slightly, the boxes looking as if they were ready to slide from the shelves. In fact, it looked as if they *were* sliding, just slowly...

A box fell to the ground near Emily, making her jump and scream, the thud so loud that it felt as if it had shaken her bones.

Then another box fell. Then another.

Emily jumped into the forklift, knowing that she would be safe with protection above her before she drove slightly, pushing the shelves back into position. They were tilting to the other side ever so slightly, but it wasn't drastic. It was better than having extremely heavy boxes raining on top of her.

After taking a moment to confirm that nothing else would fall, Emily slid out of the forklift and shakily made her way to the other side of the shelves before approaching the box.

Emily grabbed it and pulled gently, sliding it from the beam. It fell the ground... directly onto her right foot.

Emily yelped in pain, having heard a giant crunch before she agonisingly pulled her foot from underneath the box, having had to push against it in order to do so, pushing it against the bottom of the shelves.

The shelves began to tip, leaning towards her. Emily dropped to the ground in pain, unaware of what was happening. She clutched her ankle, touching even her shoe resulting in pain.

Emily didn't see the giant, heavy box falling towards her head.

Chapter 6

Emily woke up with a groan, a pressurised feeling pulsating within her skull. She'd been crushed. Brilliant.

After pulling her sleeping mask and earmuffs from her head, Emily grabbed her phone and stopped it from vibrating, continuing to lay in her bed for a few moments. The situation was beginning to annoy her slightly. She'd been aware of this oddity for four days, had died five times, and was still no closer to not only breaking the chain but figuring out why the chain was wrapped around her in the first place.

Emily went to slide out of bed but found that she didn't want to move. She felt as if the situation was depressing her, removing all will to do anything at all. She felt weak and hopeless.

"I'll try staying here again," Emily murmured to herself before realising that she'd chocked to death last time. Was that guaranteed to happen again if she would stay at home? Or could she avoid it by not going back to bed, or maybe by avoiding food altogether?

Emily pulled her phone to her face, selected her manager's contact and pulled the phone to her ear. She wasn't going to act ill this time. She was going to be honest by explaining how drained she felt.

"Hello?" Came her manager's cheery voice, making Emily smile slightly.

"Hey, I don't think that I can face work today," Emily let out, the tone of her voice shocking her slightly. She wasn't forcing anything out, so the fact that she sounded so flat just confirmed that the situation was beginning to take its toll on her.

"How come?" The manager replied, her voice elevating in pitch, sounding slightly concerned and unintentionally whiny.

"I've hit a low, to be honest," Emily explained. "Can't face getting out of bed."

"Oh dear," the manager replied, making Emily smile slightly as she couldn't recall anyone using that phrase within the previous ten years of her life. It reminded her of how her father would react whenever she'd hurt herself, giving her a tight hug and muttering the phrase before going on to patch the injury as best as possible. "Let me know if you can face work tomorrow. If not, I can put you in touch with a friend of mine. She's a great therapist- might be able to help."

"Thanks," Emily replied, touched by her managers will to help her. "I'll let you know."

"Okay," the manager replied. "Hope you feel better tomorrow!"

The call ended, leaving Emily to ponder what to do. The first thing which she wondered was whether much would change if she'd avoid a lie-in, but then her thoughts drifted to whether she was destined to choke to death on her food, whether that would happen at a specific time, whether she could avoid death at all by avoiding all food. All of the possibilities rushing through Emily's head felt like too much to take in at once, but she quickly decided on what to do: she would live through the day as she had before without going back to bed. When it would get to lunchtime, she'd focus on each mouthful and take smaller bites. If she'd end up chocking to death, she'd know whether the death was avoidable or not, would know if there was anything which she could do or whether she would have to either return to work or go through the day without eating anything.

Emily slid out of her bed and made her way to the kitchen, quickly making her breakfast before plonking herself in front of the TV.

As she'd done previously, she ate and watched the television before remaining there until lunch, getting up to make herself a sandwich, though she stopped herself before doing so. Before, she'd made two sandwiches and had chocked on the second. If she'd only make one…

Emily finished making the sandwich and stood in the kitchen to eat it, hoping that being upright would lessen the chance of chocking, hoping that focusing on each bite and only having one sandwich would annihilate the chance altogether.

With every, small bite, Emily focused, chewing slowly, making sure that the food would become extremely soft and mushy before swallowing.

Emily made it through half of the sandwich before she began chocking again.

Emily immediately tried to cough to dislodge the food, but the sliminess of the chewed sandwich had allowed it to travel much further down her windpipe, too far to get it out by simply coughing.

After throwing the top of her back against the kitchen counter, hoping to jolt it from the path towards her lungs, Emily collapsed, her back in extreme pain. She might have broken or fractured the top of her spine.

She still chocked, her body gasping for air, jolting over and over, only using more and more oxygen by doing so.

It didn't take very long for Emily to go completely still.

Emily jolted awake immediately as if a switch had been flipped and she'd gone back in time within nanoseconds. She threw her sleeping mask and her earmuffs from her head before letting out a long sigh. Dead. Again.

After silencing the vibrations of her phone and sliding out of bed, Emily moved to pull her work clothes on. From what she could see, there wasn't any point in trying to stay home again. It looked as if eating anything around lunchtime would kill her and, even then, trying to eat at all would most likely result in the same fate. She could avoid eating at all costs, of course, but would that change a lot? It was something which she could try later on, but Emily had a better idea in mind…

The second time when she'd died had been

entirely avoidable. She'd drowned in the bath. All which she had to do was avoid taking a bath. She'd go through her day as she had then, spending a little more time at the check-out than in the aisles but not making too much of an effort to be overly sociable.

Emily moved to her make-up table to brush her hair and conceal the spot on her face without even bothering to look in the mirror. She couldn't be entirely bothered to conceal the forming spot, but she had originally and, scared that changing too much would result in something drastic being altered and leading her down the wrong path, she concealed the bump.

Breakfast, TV, teeth, coat, out of the apartment. Emily descended the stairs, stepped onto the street and began the journey to work. What had she done that day exactly? All which she could remember was that she'd spent a little more time working in the check-out area during the day, that she'd stayed late for five minutes as she was scared about being hit by that car, thinking that simply leaving later would solve the problem of her dying. What else? Had she spoken to anyone in particular? She'd interacted with the creepy, old man, and realising that made Emily frown and shiver slightly, but at least she knew how to play her cards: take the money which he'd offer her. Once she'd do that, she'd be in the clear, right? Was that man some type of turning point? Did it matter how the rest of her morning was? Could she accept that man's money and stay late, then that would put her on the right route? She hoped so, scared that she'd forget to do something specific, banishing her to the fate of being struck by a car, murdered or something else just as horrible.

Emily crossed the road, entering the car park of the shop, entering the shop a minute later and making her way towards the break room to clock-in.

Emily's day was exactly the same as the day which she was trying to imitate, at least the major occurrences. She breezed through the day, constantly reminding herself not to stray from her original actions, eventually making it to the end of her shift. As she had before, she stayed for another five minutes, browsing the aisles to look for things which she could buy with her employee discount, passing the time as quickly as possible before it was time to go.

Emily timed her exit to the minute, stepping into the car park and beginning to walk home. As she had previously, she made sure to be extra careful on her way home, not too scared about being hit by a vehicle as she knew that, provided that she'd done everything correctly, she was due to die in the bath.

When Emily entered her apartment, she felt drawn to the idea of a bath. She wasn't sweating, she wasn't hot, but, for some reason, the idea of letting herself soak in a hot both felt... inviting.

No, Emily told herself mentally, being stern with herself. She didn't know why the impulse was there. It was strange, like she was destined to drown, or something.

Emily fought against the urge, taking her coat to her room to hang in her wardrobe before flopping onto the couch, turning the TV on, not knowing what else to do to pass the time. She knew that she would have to eat at some point, though she was slightly scared that she would end up setting fire to something and burning to death. Still, though, she was hungry, so it wouldn't hurt to eat *something*, would it?

When it turned seven in the evening, Emily stood and made her way to her kitchen, not knowing what to eat and so resorting to pasta. She made sure to be extra careful when cooking, staying at least one foot away from the side of the stove, petrified that she would knock the pot over and send the boiling water into her face. No such thing occurred, however, Emily dumping the slightly al dente pasta into a bowl before lightly drizzling the simple tomato sauce on top of it, taking a step back once she'd placed everything which needed washing into the sink as if trying to confirm that nothing would jump out and attack her.

After a moment, as soon as Emily felt comfortable to move, she grabbed a fork and her meal before returning to the couch to eat, making sure to focus on each mouthful of pasta as she ate.

Once Emily had finished her meal, surprised that she hadn't chocked to death, she placed the bowl and the fork into the sink, smiling to herself, proud. She was nearly there! If she wanted, she could just go to bed right then and there but, being honest with herself, she felt hesitant to do so. Emily guessed that the nightmare, the curse, whatever it was would disappear at midnight, at the beginning of the next day, and going to bed early would be ignoring the possibility of dying within the last few hours. What if she'd simply fall out of bed and crack her skull on her bedside table? There was the possibility, and that petrified Emily.

She decided to stay up, pacing around her living room lightly, bored. There wasn't anything interesting on the TV, she'd browsed through social media so much that she'd ended up looking at posts which she'd already seen, and her phone didn't have enough storage to house any games on it. She wasn't much of a reader or a gamer, so she didn't have any other entertainment to partake in. She could clean, but she was tired, and she couldn't even go to bed yet!

After a moment, Emily decided to clean her teeth. It was something to do, so why not?

Emily walked into her bathroom, letting out a sigh as she did so, contemplating what she could do to pass the time, wondering if she could spend time with a friend, or something, before she slipped at the perfect opportunity to slam her head into the sink, smashing a portion of the bowl before she head thudded on the ground.

Emily's vision faded.

Chapter 7

Emily woke up and immediately let out a groan before slowly removing her sleeping mask and earmuffs. Dead. Again. It was like a curse which she couldn't escape. Well, maybe she could escape from it by surviving until midnight, but she'd just been so close and had failed.

Staring at her ceiling, Emily knew that surviving until midnight was the answer. What else would work? But, even then, what if it wasn't possible? What if she'd been condemned to some sort of hell?

She slid from bed, contemplating what to do. She'd been so close, yet she hadn't succeeded. Did that mean that the route wouldn't work? Maybe she could try going to bed instead of staying up. What danger would she face by doing so? Yes, something stupid could happen, she could fall out of bed and crack her skull open on the side of her bedside table as she'd been thinking about before, but what were the chances? She'd stayed in bed for about an extra two hours before and she hadn't died, so...

After pulling her work clothes on, brushing her hair and concealing her spot, eating breakfast and watching the TV, Emily grabbed her coat from her wardrobe and left the house, heading in the direction of the shop.

The day panned-out exactly the same as it had previously. She mimicked herself, copying every detail which she could remember until she'd gotten home, stepping into her apartment, hoping against all odds that she'd be able to survive.

Emily walked to the stove and turned it on after having filled a pot with tap water. She placed the pot on top of the hob, her stomach cramping slightly, telling her that she was hungry, demanding food. She guessed that it wouldn't hurt to eat something as she'd eaten previously though, to be fair, she'd eaten at some point after seven, so maybe eating straight after having gotten home from work wasn't the best idea...

Emily gave up on the idea of food, taking a step away from the stove and shaking her head lightly as if trying to reason with her stomach, telling it why it wouldn't be a good idea to eat.

"I'm going straight to bed," Emily said out loud to herself as if clarifying that it was sensible.

She turned and strutted into her bedroom, holding her breath as she walked, scared that something would occur during the tiny journey to her bed. Nothing. There wasn't anyone waiting to murder her, the roof didn't collapse on her head... all which she needed to do was to undress and to climb into bed.

Emily closed the door and began to strip down to her underwear- which was what she would wear to sleep- and slid into bed, cautiously leaning back and into the pillow, pulling the crumpled duvet to her chin.

It took a few moments of scared wondering for Emily to close her eyes, feeling safe. She grabbed her sleeping mask and her earmuffs from her bedside table, pulling them on. She couldn't be bothered to set an alarm. Maybe she'd just stay asleep forever.

It barely took any time at all for Emily to fall asleep.

When Emily awoke, she crinkled her nose slightly. Smoke. The distinct smell of smoke.

She threw her sleeping mask and earmuffs from her head. The smoke alarm was blaring. She hadn't heard it because of the earmuffs!

Emily jolted out of bed and quickly glanced at her phone on her bedside table. It was only six in the afternoon! Six! She somehow had to survive for another six hours in a burning apartment!

Emily moved to the door and grabbed the handle, immediately pulling her hand away due to the searing pain of the heat. The fire was right on the other side of the door.

Taking a step back, scared, not knowing what to do, Emily began to ponder about what could have caused the fire... The stove! She'd left the stove on underneath the pan! The water must have evaporated from the heat, then the pan must have become hotter and hotter until it had caused something to catch fire... How had she been so stupid to forget to turn the stove off?

Emily backed into the far corner, whimpering silently. She had no idea about what to do. She didn't have any way to access water. Had there been any nearby, she'd have dampened a shirt and used it to cover her nose and mouth while making her way to the front door. But, then again, wasn't the fire right on the other side of her bedroom door? She probably didn't have a chance of making a run for it, at least without having to sustain serious burns while doing so. What else could she do?

Emily looked around her room frantically, searching for inspiration. Her eyes landed on her window, but what good would her window do? The drop on the other side was way too much: three storeys. She couldn't take that fall and survive. She'd probably have better odds trying to run through the fire.

After realising that she didn't have an option, Emily rushed to her wardrobe, pulling the cabinet open and beginning to wade around for anything thick enough to protect her hand. She grabbed a hoodie which she hadn't worn in months and quickly enveloped her right hand in the fabric before rushing to her bedroom door. She took a quick breath of the somewhat clean air before grabbing the door handle and pulling the door open.

The fire was right there, maybe a foot away at most. Emily staggered back immediately, the heat surprising and overwhelming her. She didn't have enough time to grab the door and to close it again, the fire advancing on the murky carpet, gliding towards her at a frightening pace.

Emily backed away from the fire before she

caught sight of her phone. She jumped for it, grabbing it before pulling back and away from the door. She began to dial for the fire brigade, but she didn't have any signal. Why didn't she have any signal?! Of all of the times... And, anyway, why weren't there firefighters getting her out already? The fire couldn't have been going on for any less then fifteen minutes for her apartment to be in its current state, so why hadn't anyone stormed in and put the blaze out?

Maybe it's a punishment for me being reckless, Emily wondered, letting out a sigh. Dying and waking up again at the beginning of the day over and over again was hardly normal. It made the idea of the fire brigade being irresponsible seem like the basic concept of physics. She wouldn't have an easy way out, or she wouldn't have a way out at all. It was entirely possible that she was destined to die, to burn to death.

Emily began to search her room for anything. The fire had started to make its way in. The corner of her bedside table which was the closest to the door was being struck by sparks of flame. Within a few minutes, the room would be ablaze, Emily included.

The room was filling with smoke, too. Emily dropped to the floor, laying on her stomach, sobbing to herself between the burning coughs and chocking. Of all of the ways which she'd died so far, this had to have been the worst way. Being hit by that car had been so unexpected that she hadn't processed what was going on. Drowning had been peaceful as she'd been asleep. Being murdered had been scary, though it had been quick. Chocking to death wasn't pleasant, but at least it was more uncomfortable than painful. Being crushed by a giant, heavy box had been quick, and that was also the case with slipping and cracking her skull open. All of her deaths had either been quick or uncomfortable. Not this. Not burning. Not having her flesh cook and melt while she would have to feel every ember of the attacking inferno.

Unable to comprehend the knowledge that she was probably going to die, Emily held the hoodie to her face, hoping that breathing through the fabric would be able to filter some of the smoke from her oxygen as she forced herself to stand up and rush to the window. Maybe there was a soft landing outside. She'd seen it done before in films: the firefighters setting up a giant inflatable target for people to jump into. Maybe something like that would be outside.

Emily gazed out of the window, straining to look down the alleyway between her apartment building and whatever building was next to it. Nothing. Maybe she could climb down…

It took a moment of consideration to rule that out. While Emily was starting to feel slightly desperate, having tried over and over to survive yet having failed… Maybe all which she had to do was to survive the fire. Maybe she'd be free then. And while that idea seemed promising, likely to be the truth as Emily didn't have any other leads to follow, she knew what would likely happen: she'd slip and fall to her death, then she'd wake up and have to figure out what to try next.

Emily backed away from the window, feeling adrenaline in her system. She wanted to run as far away as possible, wanted to fight the fire... Maybe that was what she'd have to do.

Emily looked at the open door. The fire had spread into the room slightly. Her bedside table had been set ablaze at the bottom, and the flames were licking in the direction of her bed. The bedframe would go up, and the mattress alongside the duvet and the pillows would burn very quickly and fill the room with so much smoke that Emily wouldn't have a chance of surviving. She would either have to make a run for it and hope for the best, or she would have to sit and suffocate before burning to death if the smoke wouldn't kill her first. It probably wouldn't matter that she'd suffer from terrible burns. She'd probably die, but if she'd miraculously live, maybe life would return to normal as if nothing had happened. The situation was too strange to be anything *but* a lucid nightmare, so she'd probably just wake up in reality without any injuries after breaking free of the odd curse.

It took a moment of psyching-up to do, but Emily rushed towards the door, sprinting with the hoodie pressed firmly against her nose and mouth. She burst through the door, feeling the searing pain of the flames nipping at her ankles like vicious dogs with rabies.

Emily couldn't see due to the smoke, so she had to rely on her muscle memory to traverse through the living area of her apartment. But, even then, she hadn't ever been running through her apartment, so she wasn't sure if she'd be able to correctly map everything out.

She took a few strides towards the kitchen, trying to be as fast and accurate as possible, not wanting to sacrifice either factor in the slightest. The pain... It burned so much. It felt as if her feet were going to melt. Maybe they were.

Emily turned in the direction of the front door and rushed forwards, knowing that she wouldn't be able to bare standing in an inferno for much longer, though she collided with something and promptly fell into it. The couch.

She landed on the top of it before rolling onto the seat. Emily couldn't help crying out, throwing the hoodie away as her arms flailed around, trying to get a grip underneath her, trying to push herself back to her feet. She sucked in a gargantuan amount of smoke, spluttering afterwards, trying her best to get rid of it and to get the oxygen which she needed into her lungs to replace the disgusting taste of the smoke and of the ash which had started to build-up on her tongue since she'd dropped the hoodie.

Emily ended up rolling onto the floor, screaming in pain, crying for help. She could feel tears rolling from her eyes, but they evaporated on her cheeks. Then her eyes dried.

Crying tearlessly and silently as Emily could tell that her throat and lungs had been burned so badly that she had no hope of being able to not only talk but to breathe again, she leaned into the floor, practically embracing the fact that she was going to die, knowing that there wasn't any way for her to escape the fate. Even if there *was* a way, how would she be able to survive for another six hours with horrible burns, practically melted skin, no voice or no reliable way to breathe?

A molten feeling overtook Emily's mind as the fire burned at her face. Her skin was peeling off or melting, either one, her eyes were shrivelling up like wilting flowers, making her completely blind. She felt no extra pain, already dealing with too much to handle.

Emily passed out as the flames continued to dance around her like a tribe having found a meal.

Chapter 8

Emily woke up gasping for breath, throwing her hands to her face to feel her skin, then she ran her hands around her body. Her skin was there. There weren't any burns. She was alive, at least, and she was back in her bed again. She'd been slightly scared when burning to death that the mutilation of her body would be permanent, but that wasn't the case, clearly.

She ripped the sleeping mask and the earmuffs from her head, taking a moment to think about what to do. It seemed as if going to work would always lead to a dead end. She'd been hit by a car, had drowned, had been murdered, had been crushed, had cracked her skull open, had burned to death... What else would come from attending work? Nothing good, that seemed certain.

Even though, yes, there was the possibility that Emily could go through with the day exactly the same and that she could force herself not to turn the stove on, she'd probably end up dying anyway. There was a clear track-record which illustrated the fact that she would end up dying over and over if she would try to elaborate on a workday.

Emily grabbed her phone from her chest,

silenced the vibrating alarm and moved to call her manager. She couldn't think of anything else to do, so she was going to stay home. This time, however, she wasn't going to eat anything. *Anything*. She would sit on her couch and watch TV until the day would end. Where was the danger in that?

"Hello?" Came from the phone, Emily's manger speaking with the exact same tone which she'd previously had in this situation.

"Hey, I'm not feeling too good," Emily stated immediately, not wanting to have to pretend to be ill. "I think I'll have to stay home today."

"How come?" Her manger questioned, sounding genuinely concerned as she had done previously, making Emily smile lightly again as she felt as if someone was supporting her through her incredibly uncertain time.

"Well, I've hit a low depression-wise," Emily said, not feeling as if she needed to elaborate much as the words spoke for themselves. "I can't face leaving my apartment, to be honest."

"Oh dear!" The manager let out, almost making Emily laugh a little, hearing the phrase for the second time in years. "Let me know if you can face work tomorrow. If not, I can put you in touch with a friend of mine. She's a great therapist- might be able to help."

"Thanks," Emily said, smiling to herself as if hoping that her manager could see her appreciation through the camera of her phone despite the fact that one was facing in the wrong direction and that the other was obscured by her blonde hair.

"Okay."

The call ended and Emily let out a sigh before she went to slide out of bed. She stopped herself, however, realising that she could simply stay in bed and sleep for a little longer. Yes, she'd done that before and had ended up dying, but she'd chocked to death. That had nothing to do with sleeping, so would there be any harm? Plus, Emily realised, she couldn't really face the idea of sitting in front of the TV for sixteen hours, just waiting while time would tick-by. Sleeping for a little longer would at least reduce the torturous amount of time which she would have to spend watching low-budget shows.

Emily grabbed her sleeping mask and earmuffs, pulling them back on and letting out a light, content sigh as she leaned back into her pillow. She felt comfortable. Maybe she could stay in bed all day.

It didn't take very long for Emily to fall asleep, and she only remained unconscious for two hours, pulling her sleeping mask and earmuffs from her head to check the time after her eyes had flickered open. She didn't feel tired in the slightest, convincing her that she wouldn't be able to get away with falling asleep for any longer.

She slid from her bed and slowly pulled her clothes on, almost taking pleasure in the fact that she was taking her time, reducing how long she would have to spend watching TV. She even sat at her make-up table and brushed her hair, sitting there for at least three minutes, making sure that there wasn't a single knot in sight. Emily even contemplated the idea of going for a shower. She could wash her hair, condition it thoroughly and spend a while drying it before returning to her make-up table to spend just as long brushing it again, but she ruled it out when she realised that there was the awful risk of slipping and splitting her head open.

Reluctantly, Emily stood up and dawdled as she walked from her bedroom and into the living room, moving towards the couch where she flopped down. Maybe she could try closing her eyes for a little bit to see if she could go back to sleep? Even though there wasn't a chance of Emily falling unconscious without wearing her sleeping mask and her earmuffs, she considered the idea for a moment before ruling it out. If she *could* fall asleep for a bit, it would be best to save that opportunity for later as a break from the TV.

She grabbed the remote and switched the device on, spending a few moments sliding between the free channels in search of something which peaked her attention. As soon as she'd found a show which interested her, she sat back, placed the TV remote on the arm of the chair, and began to watch.

The feeling of laziness almost immediately overwhelmed Emily as she sat there. She found her eyes drifting away from the screen occasionally, searching for something else to do. She could clean, but there was a risk of finding a way to die and, even then, the apartment probably wouldn't stay clean into reality if she'd break the death-chain. Emily could only guess what the rules of her situation were, but assumed that one of them was that changes wouldn't spill into reality. She could probably murder people in an effort to stay alive and return to reality without the event having *really* happened, meaning that doing anything productive like cleaning the apartment would only be overridden. Even though it was something else to do, Emily didn't want to risk impaling herself on the handle of the vacuum.

The show dragged on and on and on. Emily began to wonder what she was even watching, her attention fading away from the show so often that she had no clear picture of the plot. Maybe it was all rubbish anyway, random things conjured by her mind as her situation clearly wasn't reality. Maybe the show was boring because she *expected* it to be boring? Maybe she could make it more enthralling with enough belief that it would be but, then again, she'd tried to alter what was going on around her before, believing the situation to be a lucid dream where she could bend the rules of reality to her liking, but she hadn't succeeded. Maybe she hadn't focused enough, but from what she'd heard about lucid dreams in the past, all which was really required would be the knowledge that the situation is definitely a dream.

An hour passed in total, Emily letting out an elongated groan as soon as she'd noticed that barely any time had passed at all. It felt as if days had passed, it made reliving the deaths which she'd already experienced feel appealing. The show wasn't good, that was clear.

Emily switched to a different channel. It was a sports channel. She didn't have much on an interest in sports. She'd only had first-hand experience with *any* of them when she'd been forced to play them during P.E lessons in school, so she didn't have much hope of her attention being grasped by what was going on. Still, though, she had to give it a shot. It definitely seemed better than returning to the nonsense show which she'd been enduring.

Ten minutes passed before Emily had to change to another channel. She didn't really understand what was going on, had no idea about the rules and, therefore, couldn't find much enjoyment in watching people playing baseball.

She landed on the news channel, immediately moving on as she didn't want to bore herself with news which probably wasn't true. As she flicked by, she noticed a headline saying something about a coma, but she didn't want to go back to see what it was going on about.

From the news channel to another, disgustingly low-budget and unentertaining show which Emily tried to captivate herself with for twenty minutes, then back to what she'd been watching originally, letting out a long sigh. She was in for a rough day, that was for certain.

It took another hour of sitting on her couch and watching the boring show for something new to occur.

The TV screen began to flicker slightly, capturing Emily's attention as she gazed at it, confused. Horizontal, green bars appearing, flashing quickly while moving up and down. More and more appeared until they had almost covered the entirety of the screen. The audio of the TV cut off suddenly, being replaced by the very faint sound of static buzzing. Then the screen turned off entirely.

Emily, confused and very surprised, grabbed the remote and turned the TV off. She waited for a moment before she tried to turn it back on again. The red light at the bottom of the screen changed to blue to signify that it was on, but the screen remained black.

She stood up, feeling both excited and incredibly annoyed. Her only means of entertainment had just broken, but taking it to be fixed was something to do, at least.

But Emily dropped back onto the couch. *I'll probably die trying to get it fixed*, she realised, her stomach dropping. It wouldn't be worth the risk of carrying the device down the stairs, taking it to the nearest repair shop and waiting for it to be repaired. And, even then, it would probably take a few days to be repaired, so she'd still be stranded with nothing to do. Trying to get it fixed would just be a risk for nothing.

Emily leaned back into the couch, feeling uncertain about what to do. She was bored. So, so bored, but she knew that she couldn't take the TV to be repaired. Without having it repaired, she'd have nothing to do except for sitting on her couch, though. Well, she had her phone, at least.

Fifteen minutes of scrolling through social media passed before Emily had run out of things to do. She didn't play games and didn't have any space on her phone to download any, so she was stranded with nothing to do.

With a sigh, unable to resist the lovely idea of having something to do, Emily stood up and walked towards the TV, gazing at it for a moment. Maybe the problem wasn't so bad that it would require someone experienced to fix it. Maybe she just had to hit the top of it to get it working again.

Emily tried that, smacking the top of the device and taking a step back to gaze at the screen. Nothing. It wasn't that simple.

She grabbed the TV remote and turned the device off with a light sigh as she processed that she was really going to risk the chance of death just because she was bored. Though, to be fair, she wasn't entirely certain that she wouldn't die of boredom by sitting in her living room with nothing to do for hours upon hours on end.

Emily approached the wall, reaching her arm around blindly, feeling for the extension lead. Once she'd unplugged what she could only guess was the TV, she went to pick it up, pulling it into the air and taking a step backwards.

A sudden amount of resistance yanked the TV back, pulling Emily with it and to the ground. The TV fell to the floor, Emily beside it, her heart beating faster and faster as she realised that there had been a chance for her to have been crushed by the device.

Confused and curious as to why the TV had seemingly launched itself back into the direction of the wall, Emily looked down the back of the cabinet which it had been residing on, seeing the extension lead. She'd unplugged the wrong thing.

Emily let out a deep breath, relieved that her mistake hadn't caused her to die, when she noticed that the cover of the wall-plug which had the extension lead plugged into it had come off, still connected to the wiring of the apartment.

Scared that leaving the wires dangling out of the wall would start another fire, Emily grabbed the cover and put it back into position, though her finger grazed one of the live wires.

Emily was propelled backwards and to the floor, her breath shocked out of her, quite literally as the electricity had stunned her lungs, stopping them from taking in oxygen. Even thinking about getting her lungs working again didn't work.

Emily tried to breathe, tried to focus on getting her respiratory system functioning again, but she realised that she couldn't move anything. She was paralysed.

Petrified of what was to follow, Emily tried to fight against the paralysis, though found that she couldn't move no matter what. Her breathing hadn't returned and, she realised, she needed CPR, yet there wasn't anyone around to give her the treatment which she so desperately required to stay alive and not to fail another attempt at escaping the hellhole of her vicious cycle.

Emily tried again and again, but nothing happened. Not until her vision faded and she fell unconscious, at least.

Chapter 9

Emily let out a long sigh as soon as her eyes had opened and she saw the darkness which came with her vision being blocked by the sleeping mask. Dead. Again. The ninth death in total, the eighth variety.

After pulling the sleeping mask and the earmuffs from her head, Emily began to ponder what to do. Going to work seemed like a dead end. Staying at home seemed like a dead end. What else could she do? Skipping work seemed like it *could* be the answer, but staying at home to do so seemed like the wrong idea... Maybe she could skip work but go somewhere else, somewhere which would be safe, somewhere that she could trust. But she didn't know of anywhere like that in the city. She couldn't exactly go to a coffee shop, or something, and stay there for the entire day, so what *could* she do? She could wander around, maybe, but there was the risk of being hit by cars or being caught in a situation which would kill her. But, then again, Emily didn't have another idea.

Unable to come up with anything else, Emily grabbed her phone and turned the vibrating alarm off before moving to her contact list to find her manager.

Emily went through with the same conversation

which she'd been a part of three times now, telling her manager that she felt extremely low, asking for the day off, being given the time off and the call ending without much else going on. She then slid out of bed and pulled some clothes on, brushed her hair, concealed the spot which was still trying to form on her left cheek and left her bedroom, making sure to grab her phone on the way out before she entered her kitchen, beginning to make herself some toast for her breakfast.

Emily didn't watch TV while eating- consuming her breakfast by the toaster instead- as she felt drained of watching the same, terrible show which she'd seen countless times over and over again. She finished eating, placed her plate into the sink, and then wondered what she could do that day. She was going to wander around, but where would she go? Would she really just let herself wander, or would it be a much better idea to plan to visit a few, time-consuming locations?

Despite living there, Emily didn't know the city very well. It wasn't too far away from where she'd grown up, but it wasn't overwhelmingly close, either. She hadn't moved-in very long before, and she'd never had a proper chance to explore the city, something which meant that she had no idea about what to do and, on top of that, something which confused her when it came to what she would find. She was probably in a lucid nightmare as she'd previously deduced, so how would she know what was in the city? She wouldn't, obviously, meaning that her mind would have to make everything up. Maybe she could look online for a map of the city and they'd correspond perfectly, but there wasn't any guarantee of everything being... normal. Her situation wasn't normal in the slightest, so what were the chances of her walking in a direction which she hadn't been in before and seeing a regular city? Things could be entirely off from what she perceived and normal, maybe making everything worse for her situation. She could stumble across a wild-west type of place and be shot for trespassing, she could walk right into the middle of a dystopian reality and be mauled to death by zombies. The possibilities were endless and, as a result, terrifying.

Emily walked to her bedroom, retrieved her coat from her wardrobe, then made sure that she had everything with her before walking out of her apartment, locking the door behind her and beginning to head down the stairs. Once she'd stepped onto the street, Emily immediately began to head in the opposite direction of her workplace.

Not much was very different. She'd seen the street which she was walking down before, knew that it didn't have much to offer but that it led to the much more interesting centre of the city. Emily had about a twenty-minute walk ahead of her, something which seemed frightening at the beginning as there was the very clear possibility of meeting another fate during the journey, but she eventually forgot the risk which she was facing and walked, her mind preoccupied with taking in her surroundings.

Once the journey was complete and Emily had

stepped onto what must have usually been the busiest street in the city, she couldn't help the light smile which had appeared on her face. She didn't know what it was exactly, but standing on a street which was much quieter than usual just seemed to calm her. Maybe it was a sense of tranquillity that resonated with her situation, like a calmer atmosphere would help her to overcome her problem.

Emily made her way to a nearby coffee shop almost immediately, thinking that it would be a good place to spend half-an-hour while she would contemplate what to do. The street had plenty of shops which she could spend her time looking around, knowing that there wasn't going to be much of a danger in any of them, but she didn't want to spend the whole day only exploring aisles. She thought that she'd spotted an arcade at one end of the street and, given that it was the middle of the week, it would be fairly quiet in there. Maybe she could spend some time roaming around the inside of the arcade before it would undoubtedly start to get busier and busier.

After ordering a coffee and dropping into a seat with the Styrofoam cup in her hand, Emily closed her eyes for a moment and let out a sigh before going to take a sip of the coffee, halting herself when she realised that she would only burn her mouth.

Even though she wasn't at home or at work, something felt slightly hopeless around her, like her mind *knew* that she was going to die at some point and, Emily noted solemnly, *she* knew that, too. It was almost an obligation to suffer from death, she realised. The question which prodded her was the idea of when the death would occur and what it would be. Then there was the question of whether or not it would be preventable.

Stop it, she shunned herself mentally before subconsciously raising her arm and sipping the coffee in her hand, burning her tongue slightly as she'd expected would happen. *Just go with the day*.

And that was exactly what Emily did.

After finishing her coffee, Emily walked out of the coffee shop and made her way to the arcade, hoping to pass some time there. She bought a few tokens and started to walk around, looking for anything which interested her. Memories would flood back occasionally from her high-school years. She could remember that she and her friends would spend some time at an arcade because there was a popular girl in their school who loved gaming and they wanted to get to know her, hoping that they would be able to climb the social ladder a little. It had worked in the end, though not as well as Emily and her friends had initially hoped. They'd become a little more recognised, yes, but they realised that the popular girl wouldn't talk about her arcade friends very much to the other popular girls. At the time, Emily didn't know why and craved to know the reason, feeling slightly frustrated that she wasn't getting the recognition which she'd hoped to receive, but, as an adult, she could see that the girl was most likely afraid to admit that she liked something which, at the time, was commonly associated with nerds and geeks more than the pretty and popular girls who dominated the social-food-chain.

A few of the games which Emily played were ones which she'd played previously, feeling jabs of nostalgia strike her when she would see them or realise that she'd played them before. She ended up having much more fun than she'd initially expected before she left as lunchtime was approaching.

Emily went to a fast-food chain, wanting something comforting and cheap to devour as she realised that the money which she'd brought with her would have to last for as long as possible lest she'd have no choice but to wander home, doomed with entertaining herself with terrible TV.

After eating, Emily began to make her way down the street, looking at shops which interested her on her way past. She wasn't being particularly fussy with the ones which she would enter giving that she had a long, long time to spend wandering around, but she made sure not to bore herself, only entering the somewhat interesting places. One shop sold what Emily could only describe as relics from the early eighties, anything which looked slightly outdated. One such item which caught her attention was an electric guitar which had been graffitied slightly, one of the volume knobs having fallen off, too.

It didn't take very long for Emily to grow tired of her aimless browsing. After checking her phone to see just how much time had passed, she saw that it was nearing two in the afternoon. Guessing that it would be a good idea to head home at six to ensure that there wasn't a chance of being caught in a rush-hour and to make sure that she wouldn't go home too early, having to resort to terrible entertainment to pass the last few hours, Emily decided to visit another coffee shop to kill a little bit of time while figuring out something to do.

She'd strayed from the initial street which she'd found slightly, not having travelled too far, though she was far enough away that she couldn't see a direct route back to it. Even though she'd been doing a bit more walking, however, Emily hadn't seen anything interesting. The city almost seemed to repeat itself, shops, more shops, the occasional restaurant or coffee shop, houses, blocks of flats, the occasional bar, casino, arcade or bank, but nothing else. Emily wasn't a gambler and, even if she was, she didn't have the money to spend on it. She thought that it would a terrible idea to get drunk when fighting to stay alive, and she'd already played so many games at the arcade which she'd visited that she didn't have the will to play anything else for a while. She didn't need to run any errands and it was too early to get dinner, so what could she do?

Emily took her coffee to go, deciding to explore a little more. Maybe she could stumble across something interesting. Maybe she could find a park and walk around it, taking in the small amount of greenery amidst the bustling city. Maybe she could find a museum. She had a slight interest in history, after all, and while it probably wasn't enough to enthral her completely with the past, it was probably enough to aid her to pass the remaining time which she had.

Emily came to a staircase and began to descend it, wondering what the chances of finding a museum were, happy with the thought of spending two hours exploring a specific piece of history, when she tripped, her right foot catching the back of her left ankle as she leaned forwards to descend another step.

Emily's face thudded into a stone step, then her body flew into the air, bouncing from the ground, travelling down the stairs. Her back slammed into the staircase, the centre of her spine cracking as it smacked the corner of a step. She bounced again before her head thudded into the concrete of the pavement, her body landing in a heap at the bottom of the staircase, folded over itself.

Chapter 10

As usual, Emily woke up. It was slow this time. She opened her eyes and dawdled while she pulled her hands to her head to remove her sleeping mask and earmuffs. The plan which she'd been hoping would work had failed. What now? Were there *any* options left? She couldn't stay at home, she couldn't go to work, she couldn't roam the city. What *could* she do?

Maybe the city's the problem, Emily wondered, about to contemplate what she could do to solve that, though the answer was obvious: she could leave. There was a train station nearby, and she doubted that it would take so long to get out of the city that she was at high risk of dying. Something which Emily had noticed was the fact that there was a correlation between her deaths and the later parts of the day. It seemed as if she wouldn't die in the morning and, now that she was thinking about it, Emily realised that she hadn't died *once* before lunchtime. Maybe that meant that she had a safety net of about four hours to come up with a plan and to make a move. That would *definitely* be enough time to get to the train station, to get onto a train and to get out the city. She'd probably cross the border before ten in the morning, even!

Emily turned the vibrating alarm off and was about to call her manager before she paused. She'd called her each time she'd stayed off work. Maybe not letting her know that she wouldn't be going in would spark a change. But, then again, if this would fix Emily's problem, she didn't want there to be any consequences to her actions. There wasn't any proof that anything would become reality, and she'd even estimated that she'd simply wake up in reality as if the entire ordeal had been a dream, but she didn't want to take the risk. Getting out of the city was something completely new, meaning that there was a higher chance of it working than altering a previous strategy.

She called her manager, hastily explained that she felt ill as she wondered whether changing her excuse would have any effect, then clambered out of bed and began to get dressed.

After brushing her hair and dealing with the spot on her cheek, she grabbed her phone and walked to the kitchen to make a quick breakfast. She wasn't going to spend too much time getting ready as it would probably be pointless, so she just wanted to eat a slice of toast and then to get out of her apartment. If she had a safety net until lunchtime, she wanted to make the most of it.

After eating, she grabbed her coat, made sure that she had everything and proceeded to leave her apartment, rushing down the stairs and onto the street before she began to head in the direction of the shop which she worked in, the train station just a little further than it.

The walk was quiet given that the rush-hour hadn't begun. The road definitely wasn't still, but there was a significant decrease in the number of vehicles from what Emily was used to having to deal with in the morning.

As she made her way past the shop, she heard someone call her name. Startled and slightly scared, she turned to look in the direction of the shop and saw her manager checking the street for cars before she began to rush over, making her way towards Emily.

Emily paused, trying to think of an excuse. She'd said that she was ill, yet she was outside almost immediately after having called, walking away from her apartment. She needed an excuse- and quickly, too!

"What are you doing out?" Her manager asked, coming to a halt next to Emily, placing her hands on her hips and tilting her head as she stared at Emily, looking very slightly annoyed, worrying Emily as she thought that she might have blown the fact that she wasn't really ill. "You should still be in bed!"

"I-I'm going to the pharmacy," Emily stuttered slightly, trying to steady her breathing, scared that she'd give herself away. She hoped that nothing would cross-over from her situation and into reality when she'd break free, scared that she'd end up being punished for being caught. "I don't have anything at home for colds."

Her manager raised her eyebrows a little. "Nothing?" She questioned, seeming surprised. Emily grasped at the opportunity to cling to her excuse, thinking that she was on the right track to getting off of the hook.

"We have stuff in there," the manager stated, motioning towards the shop. "Stay there- I'll get something for you."

With that, she rushed towards the shop, Emily having to stand and watch as her manager made her way across the road and through the entrance.

Emily let out a light sigh, relieved. For a moment, she'd thought that she'd blown the cover of being ill, but it seemed as if everything was fine. The only problem was that she was wasting time by having to wait for her manager. And, then, she guessed, she'd have to walk back in the direction of her apartment until she wouldn't be in her manager's sight lest she'd look suspicious.

It took two minutes for Emily's manager to come out of the shop, heading back to Emily with two boxes of cold medicine in her hand. One seemed to be tablets while the other looked to be throat soothers.

"These are all I could find that'll help you," her manager stated, thrusting the two boxes into Emily's hands. "They usually help me when I get ill, so they'll probably help you, too. My immune system is terrible," she let out, laughing a little.

"Thanks," Emily said, about to pull some money from her pocket to give to her for the medicine, though her manager shook her head once she realised what Emily was doing.

"No need to pay me!" She let out, waving her hands in front of her as if frantic to get the point across.

"They're on me."

"You sure?"

"I'm fine with paying for them if it means that you'll get better quicker."

Emily smiled and waited for a moment. "Thanks," she let out.

"Now, get back to bed," her manager stated, motioning in the direction of Emily's apartment. "You don't want your cold to get worse!"

Emily nodded meekly, turning to head in the direction of her apartment. She began to make her way back slowly, waiting for a minute before glancing behind her. Her manager had disappeared, having most likely gone into the shop.

Emily continued to walk in the direction of her apartment, taking the first turning which she found, continuing down the road until she found another turning which led in the direction of the train station. She didn't want to risk passing in front of the shop again, scared of her manager seeing, so she decided to try to sneak past.

The remainder of the journey was slightly confusing as Emily didn't really know where she was going, but she eventually found her way to the train station, walking into the building and looking at a list of the locations which the trains were heading in. She didn't want to go very far, only wanted to get out of the city, hoping that doing so would halt the death-chain which she was stuck in.

Once Emily had located the cheapest price to get

out of the city, she memorised the destination and joined the queue to buy her ticket. The queue wasn't very long, so she didn't have to wait for a while, reaching the front, purchasing her ticket and being ushered towards the second platform.

Emily made her way towards the platform. The train was due to arrive within the next hour, something which she was extremely relieved about as she would still fall within her safety net, something which she realised after checking the time and seeing that it was nearing nine in the morning. She had three hours. If the train would take an entire hour to arrive- or would even be delayed by another hour- she'd still fall comfortably within her safety net.

Emily dropped onto a bench, letting out a slightly content breath as she did so. The platform was fairly busy, but it wasn't too bad. There were probably about fifty people there in total, and Emily expected that not many more would arrive, so there probably wasn't much of a danger of having to wait for the next train due to there being so many people. And, even if that ended up being the case and, for whatever reason, she was required to wait for longer, she'd still fall within her safety net, at least probably.

Time seemed to pass extremely slowly. Emily spent some time on her phone, though, due to the lack of games, she ran out of things to do very quickly, ending up having to resort to looking at the buildings which resided on the other side of the train track which was in front of her.

As time progressed, more and more people seemed to turn up, surprising Emily a little. What had initially been at most fifty people on the platform evolved to about sixty, then to seventy, then to one-hundred. Emily watched as more and more people arrived, bewildered. Why were so many people turning up? Emily wasn't catching the train to get to another city, so there was hardly a giant demand to get to the destination. How come so many people were turning up?

Maybe this platform is for two trains, Emily wondered, unsure. She shrugged very slightly to herself, trying to disregard her confusion. It wasn't a big deal. It wasn't as if she was being suffocated because there was so many people, so what was the problem?

By the time that Emily was thirty minutes into her wait, even more people had turned up. There must have been one-hundred and twenty people on the platform, all of them waiting for either Emily's train or for one which would come before or after it.

Emily began to feel slightly claustrophobic. Even though she didn't suffer from claustrophobia usually, for some reason, she had the urge to run away. It was like something was telling her to get away from the platform, some type of fear forming like a fight or flight response which urged for her to sprint out of the train station. Despite feeling the pushes of the urge, however, Emily knew to stay where she was. There wasn't much longer left, maybe only fifteen minutes, so she knew that she could remain on the bench for the remainder of the time. Or, at least, she *hoped* that she could.

Five more minutes passed and not much more changed except for the amount of people on the platform. Emily even began to count as many people as possible, curious as to the amount. One-hundred and thirty-seven was the number which she counted, though she guessed that there were more whom she couldn't see. Why were there so many? It was a weekday, early in the morning, and the destination was far from a capital city. In fact, as Emily didn't recognise the name of the place which she was going to, she guessed that it was a small place, a town which wasn't very popular or well-known, somewhere much more rural than the city. Why were so many people trying to go there? The only explanation which Emily could think of was that there was supposed to be another train arriving to go to somewhere else but, even then, why were there so many people? The train wouldn't be right behind or right in front of hers, so why were they there so early or so late?

After another five minutes, Emily had to stand up. Her legs were starting to go slightly numb, and she knew that she probably wouldn't have the space to be able to stand up when even more people would arrive. Only a few more people had funnelled into the station, but the platform was still becoming more and more cluttered. There must have been close to one-hundred and fifty people there at the very least.

When Emily finally heard the train arriving, everyone began to head towards the edge of the platform, people trying to predict where the doors would be so that they could get on and get seats. Emily also made her way to the front, realising that everyone wanted the train, realising that there was a risk of her having to wait for the next one and go through the situation again.

As Emily fought against other people to make her way to the edge of the platform, she felt herself being pushed and bounced around to the point that it reminded her of playing on a trampoline or a bouncy castle when she was younger. It was like people were *trying* to slam into her and push her in different directions.

Once Emily had finally made it to the edge of the platform, she still wasn't able to stand stably. She was being wobbled around constantly, something which scared her. She could occasionally be moved in the direction of the tracks, something which immediately boosted her adrenaline and reaction-time. She grabbed onto the wrist of a young-looking businessman to yank herself back to safety at one point, had to grab onto the arm of a middle-aged woman to keep herself from falling onto the platform. The train was getting closer and closer. It was probably only a few seconds away. She only had to keep her balance for a tiny bit longer. It wasn't too much of an ask, was it?

The train continued to get closer and, as a result, people began to push a little more.

Emily slipped onto the track, her hands barely missing the chance to grab onto the other people to keep herself stable.

She slammed onto the tracks, her head smacking into the metal and knocking her out just a few moments before the train arrived.

Chapter 11

Escaping hadn't worked. She was trapped.

That realisation hit Emily as she woke up again, her body feeling slightly warm due to the effort which she'd been putting into remaining on the platform.

Emily pulled her sleeping mask and earmuffs from her head as usual before silencing the vibrating alarm of her phone. Why hadn't it worked? Was she *really* trapped, or was catching the train the wrong way to get out? Maybe she needed to drive, walk or fly to get out of the city. But, even then, she didn't feel much hope towards the idea of those methods succeeding. It felt as if the challenge was to survive *inside* of the city, not to get out of it. Maybe she could try again later if nothing else would succeed but, laying there, Emily didn't want to make another attempt to run away. It would be good to dwell on the concept for a little longer. Maybe it was the right track but she wasn't making the right moves. Maybe she needed to wait until it was later in the day. Maybe she needed to wait until she didn't have a safety net so that it wouldn't be cut down the middle.

After sliding her legs out from under the duvet, Emily sat on her bed, her head in her hands as she wondered what to do. Going to work and staying at home still wasn't going to help, she guessed, and she'd tried to roam around the city before... Maybe she hadn't been as careful as she should have been, that being the reason why she'd died but, then again, almost all of her deaths could have been prevented simply by being a little bit more careful, so she didn't expect that walking slower or being ready to catch herself was the answer to her problem.

What if I don't go out alone? Emily wondered, realising that she hadn't tried *anything* like that before. She'd been trying to get through her attempts on her own, keeping an eye out for any possible danger, keeping track of what she needed to do to change the outcome of the day. What if she had someone beside her throughout the situation, someone who could warn her of any possibility of death? But, then again, how would she do that? She'd have to skip work, then go to a friend who wouldn't be working, convince them to spend the entirety of the day with her *and* somehow explain her situation so that they'd know to warn her of anything. Would that really work? Was she even allowed to tell people about what was going on?

Unsure as to what else she could possibly do, Emily quickly called her manager, explaining that she felt ill and that she wouldn't be in for the day before she got dressed slowly, still contemplating the thought. Who could she go to, anyway? She didn't have many friends who lived close enough that she could walk to them. Getting the train to even get across the city seemed like it wouldn't work, and she expected that trying to get a taxi would result in the same fate, the car crashing, or something. The only person whom she could think of was Brett, a friend whom she'd made in the first year of high school, someone who'd just so happened to have moved to the city not long after Emily had. He didn't live very far away, his apartment probably only a twenty-minute walk away at most, so Emily guessed that she wouldn't be killed on the way. She hadn't been killed while walking to the train station or while walking to the street which she'd spent so much time exploring, so she *probably* wouldn't be killed on the way.

Yeah, Emily thought. *That's what I'll do*.

Once Emily had finished getting dressed and had quickly brushed her hair- deciding not to bother with concealing the forming spot on her face- she went to the kitchen to quickly grab breakfast as she had the day before, eating hastily before grabbing her coat, making sure that she had everything and leaving the apartment.

As soon as she'd stepped onto the street, Emily began to make her way in the direction which she believed to be the direction of Brett's apartment. She wasn't completely certain, only having visited him there once before, but she could recognise the route which she was taking, something which assured her that she was correct.

The journey took twenty minutes before Emily was stood outside of the giant apartment building. There were at least eight floors, and Brett lived in one of the two apartments on the seventh floor, making Emily sigh a little as she was lightly out of breath from the journey and didn't like the prospect of having to trudge up so many stairs.

After entering and beginning to make her way up to the top, Emily had to pause on the stairs for a moment, leaning against the wall as she caught her breath. She began to wonder about the chances of the idea being successful, scared that she'd made the journey for no reason, but shook the idea from her mind. If Brett had something to do, she could just force him to go with her. It wouldn't be hard. He'd always been a bit of a pushover.

Emily continued the journey after having caught her breath, arriving on the seventh floor and knocking on Brett's door. It took a moment before he answered, clearly surprised to see Emily.

"Emily?" He asked, his gruff voice raising a note or two as he said her name, his blue eyes looking surprised. "What are you doing here? Don't you work today?"

Emily shrugged. "Pulling a sickie," she stated before she gave Brett a quick hug. "Wanna hang out?"

Brett looked slightly solemn for a moment. "Can't," he informed, seeming begrudging to decline. "Need to do some errands today."

"How many errands?" Emily countered, realising that she could simply tag alongside him while he'd get his chores done. "I can come with you."

"I don't think you'd like that," Brett replied with a light smirk. "They're boring."

"I'm bored, so there won't be much of a

difference," Emily argued, to which Brett paused and considered her words.

"If you're sure," he replied, shrugging slightly, his fair-length black hair bouncing a little before he motioned for Emily to enter the apartment.

Emily walked in and quickly took in the surroundings. The apartment was the same as she could recall from the last time that she'd been there, the perfect, colour-coordinated furniture seeming to fade together to form the perfect picture of a room. Brett was an interior designer, something which he'd always been strangely passionate about since Emily had first met him, though the reason had become clear when she'd discovered that he had OCD, something which made him constantly crave to perfect the tiny inconsistencies in a room. That made him a perfect fit for the job, allowing him to be hired by a company almost immediately after applying.

"So, how come you're skipping work, anyway?" Brett questioned, tilting his head slightly as he gazed at her. "You haven't done this before."

Emily paused for a moment, pondering whether or not to tell Brett the truth. Though, she realised, it would only be beneficial to do so. He could help to warn her about any danger which would arise, he'd help to shield her from everything as much as possible. Why shouldn't she explain?

"It's a bit complicated," Emily replied, pausing. Brett stared at her, eager to hear her explanation. "Basically, I'm trapped in death-loop."

"What?" Brett inquired, trying not to burst-out-laughing at the absurdity of the claim. "What's a death-loop?"

Emily shrugged, not knowing how to explain it very well. "I'm... having dreams, I suppose. I'm experiencing the same day over and over again, but I keep dying some way or another. I always wake up again and the day's exactly the same, just I'll die in a different way if I make a change."

"Like a game?" Brett questioned, beginning to catch onto the concept. "Like you're dying in a video game and respawning at a checkpoint?"

"Yeah, I guess," Emily replied, shrugging, not having played many games which included things like extra lives and checkpoints, not knowing if it was a perfect comparison or not. "Just the difficulty's at the maximum it can be."

Brett folded his arms as he looked at Emily, trying to take it in. Emily was surprised that he hadn't immediately assumed that she was joking, or something. He looked as if he believed every word which she'd said, pleasantly surprising Emily.

"So, why are you with *me*, then?" He questioned. "Trying to pass the curse onto me?" He joked, though his tone had a lace of accusation hidden within the words.

"No, no!" Emily let out, waving her hands in front of her as she denied it. "I just haven't tried spending the day with someone else yet. I was thinking that it would be safer, maybe that you're not supposed to die so there won't be much of a risk."

Brett considered that. "I suppose that makes sense," he stated, contemplating the concept before he shrugged. "I don't know, though. Anything could *still* happen, just it would kill *you* and not me. You could fall into the road, or something. That wouldn't kill me."

Emily realised that he was right but didn't want to completely admit it. She'd tried going to work, staying at home, escaping the city, and this was the only other thing which she could think of trying. She didn't want to just assume that it wouldn't work without at least *trying* it, especially given that she was working to save her life.

"I can only think to try," Emily mumbled, a giant fraction of her previous confidence in the concept having been washed away.

Brett remained silent. "Okay," he replied. "I need to do a few things here, then I need to go to the bank, go shopping, send a parcel off... I have a lot to do, so if you're *sure* that you want to spend the day with me..."

"I'm sure," Emily reassured, smiling at Brett. She didn't know if he was scared about the chance of *him* being killed as well, and if he was, she greatly appreciated the fact that he was willing to risk his life in an attempt to save her from her strange situation which had plagued her for what felt like so very long.

Emily sat on the couch while Brett got on with a few chores, cleaning the apartment, filing taxes, even gathering a box of items which he intended to donate to charity as he no longer needed them. She watched him rush around, trying to get everything done, the two of them talking to pass the time. They tried to stay away from talking about Emily's situation, Brett not wanting to worry Emily by reminding her of it.

By the time that Brett had finished the chores which he needed to do within the house, he gathered everything which he needed to take with him to get stuff done away from the apartment, gathering some money which he needed to put into his bank account, two, empty carrier bags which he'd fill with shopping and the box of items which he'd be donating to charity alongside the parcel he needed to send. Emily felt awkward being there as Brett insisted on carrying everything, thinking that she'd have a higher chance of survival if she wouldn't be weighed down by anything.

As soon as they left, Brett immediately led Emily to the nearest charity shop, dropping off the donation before they began to make their way to Brett's bank.

They walked in silence, both of them slightly on edge. Brett's head seemed to be on a swivel, looking at everything, making sure that nothing bad would happen.

Once they'd arrived at the bank, they walked in, beginning to wait in the queue as the paying-in machine was out of service.

Emily immediately noticed a girl who was stood near the front of the queue. She looked nervous for whatever reason, looking around, tapping her foot lightly. She even had a hood on even though, Emily thought, that wasn't allowed inside of the bank. Emily disregarded it, pulling her phone out to check the time. It was nearing eleven. Maybe they could get something to eat after doing the shopping.

The queue moved forwards and the nervous-looking girl stepped towards one of the workers before she shoved her hand into her pocket and pulled out a gun, pointing it at the man on the other side of the glass.

"Give me everything!" She let out, her voice slightly shaky.

A few people turned and tried to run away, but the girl quickly spun around, adrenaline clearly fuelling her movements. She pointed the gun at the man who was the closest to the door. "Leave and I'll shoot you!"

Everyone was quiet, petrified with fear.

"On the ground," she continued, motioning towards the floor with her gun.

Everyone obliged, though Brett nudged Emily lightly.

"I'm going to distract her, you run," he whispered, to which Emily stared at him, bewildered.

Emily went to reply, but Brett jumped forwards, grabbing the woman's knees and yanking her over his shoulder, making her slam into the ground as Emily jumped up from where she'd been crouching, rushing towards the door, sprinting as fast as she could, not wanting Brett's possible sacrifice to go to waste.

But a gunshot rang out and Emily collapsed to the ground.

Chapter 12

Emily immediately began to slide out of bed once her eyes had opened and she'd realised that she was starting again. She got her feet onto the floor as she removed her sleeping mask and earmuffs, her phone falling into her lap, still vibrating slightly. She grabbed it, turned the alarm off and immediately moved to call her manager.

Yes, Emily had died again, but she'd had an idea: she had been following Brett around while he was doing chores, meaning that preventing him from getting on with the tasks which he needed to complete would be altering the day drastically and, as a result, would probably have some type of desired effect. It wasn't guaranteed, of course, but Emily had a hunch that she could have a chance of survival. The idea of spending the day with someone else to have extra protection was just too good to give up on so early, even if she'd previously had doubts and even though she'd already been killed while trying to utilise the exact same strategy.

Emily hastily explained to her manager that she felt ill and that she didn't think that she could go into work, then slid out of bed and began to get ready for the day. Afterwards, she quickly ate breakfast, grabbed everything which she would need and left the house without even considering how she was going to drag Brett away from his chores. Given that he had OCD, knowing that he should do something like cleaning the house but not doing it would likely drive him insane, so how would she do it? Could she trick him into spending the day with her, or would that be too harsh? She could always explain her situation again, and maybe that would incentivise him to use as much willpower as possible to leave the tasks incomplete, but would that work?

As Emily made her way across the city and towards Brett's apartment, she contemplated what to do, eventually deciding that she could probably help with the chores if Brett would insist to get them done. With her helping, they could get the tasks done quicker and, as a result, that girl wouldn't be there when they'd get to the bank.

Emily lightly shunned herself for not being more suspicious of the girl. She'd let her guard down. Being with someone else had made her feel much more protected than she probably should have despite the doubts which she'd had earlier in the day while thinking about it. Seeing the girl in the queue, Emily had simply thought of her as nervous, maybe that she was checking-in a large sum of money and was scared of being questioned, scared of something going wrong and losing it all. Emily could identify with that as she'd felt incredibly anxious while putting the first of her money into her bank account when she'd opened it, so she hadn't questioned it as much as she definitely should have. Anyway, if Emily couldn't change anything and they'd end up in the queue of the bank with the girl there, she could at least drag Brett away and quickly explain concerns about her safety. Brett wouldn't question it, so it *could* work if it would come to it.

When Emily entered the apartment building and had made her way up the stairs, she knocked on Brett's door, waited for a moment for him to answer, then walked in as soon as the door had opened.

"What's up?" Brett questioned, taken aback slightly by Emily pushing into his apartment.

"It's complicated," Emily began, pausing for a moment before she broke into her explanation. She went over the same points which she'd previously told Brett, though made sure to also inform him that she'd tried spending time with him before and that it hadn't gone well.

"So, we need to avoid the bank, then?" Brett questioned, to which Emily nodded slowly. "Yeah," she let out, making Brett consider something. "Well, I could always go on my own in a minute. I *really* need to get these chores done, so…"

"I'll stay here while you do that, then," Emily suggested, to which Brett nodded lightly.

"Okay, I'll get the bank, the shopping, the parcel and the donation done in a minute…" he began, his voice trailing off as he rushed to gather the box which already had a few items within it, hastily placing a few others into it after a moment before he grabbed everything which he needed for the bank and before he grabbed the empty shopping bags alongside the parcel. "Stay here," Brett instructed needlessly. "And don't do anything dangerous!" He warned, backing towards the door before he turned around and left.

Emily sat in Brett's apartment while he dealt with his errands, watching the TV for what ended up being an hour. Brett had other channels compared to what she had to suffer through, so she was thoroughly entertained until he returned.

"I just need to clean the house a little, then we can do whatever you need to do," Brett informed her after having walked back into the apartment, flashing a smile in her direction as he walked to the kitchen to drop-off the shopping which he'd brought home with him.

Another hour passed with Emily simply watching the TV as Brett cleaned the house. Emily offered to help, feeling guilty that she was intruding on Brett, but he explained briefly that it would be better for the cleaning to take longer as there would be less of a chance of something going wrong and killing Emily, something which she had to agree with as she could see his argument.

Once all of Brett's chores had finally been completed, it was nearing twelve, prompting Brett to decide to make them lunch, supplying Emily with a bowl of soup not long later.

"So," he started, sitting next to her with a bowl

of his own chicken soup. "What's the plan?"

"Honestly, it's hard to come up with *any* type of plan," Emily admitted, shrugging lightly before she placed a spoonful of soup in her mouth and flapped her hand in the direction of her mouth once she'd realised that it was still very hot.

Brett suppressed a laugh at Emily before he paused to think while continuing to eat carefully. "We need to put you in a bubble, or something."

Emily was slightly amused at that though genuinely began to consider it. She was slowly running out of options, so *any* idea was welcome, really. "I've tried shielding myself in my apartment, but it hasn't worked."

Brett looked at Emily, prompting her to elaborate.

"I've ended up chocking to death and electrocuting myself," she recalled, cringing slightly at the memory of the feeling of not being able to breathe which had come with both deaths. "I've tried to stay away from home and work, but I just ended up smashing my skull on the floor," she continued, regretting saying what she had as the soup suddenly became a little less appetising.

Brett didn't seem to be affected by the image, having a bit more of his soup as he considered something. "So, if we go out *together*, what do you think'll happen?"

"Well, last time, I was shot by a bank robber," Emily reminded him, to which he shrugged.

"We could go to places where you'll be safe, places that no-one would want to steal from," he insisted.

"I *did* spend some time in a café and in an arcade," Emily recalled from the time when she'd tried to escape from her usual routine, something which seemed to finalise Brett's thought.

"We'll go to an arcade, then," he stated, to which Emily considered it and nodded. She'd had a good time when she'd played in the arcade before and, when being honest with herself, she didn't think that she'd thought about her situation while playing the various games there. It would be a good distraction, especially since she'd already made it to lunchtime *and* as she would be with Brett. They could spend two or three hours there, maybe even a little longer. It wasn't a bad idea.

"Okay," Emily agreed, smiling slightly at the appealing thought of having a chance to forget about her situation.

They finished their lunch and immediately left Brett's apartment, beginning to explore the city in search of an arcade, finding one after ten minutes of wandering around in what felt like circles.

They entered before purchasing some tokens and beginning to look around for something to play, deciding on a game which required two players to fight increasing hordes of zombies. While playing the game, Emily wondered whether she was going to have to deal with something like that for real and, when considering it, it didn't *really* seem too farfetched. She was in a death-loop, coming back to life, reliving the same day, so the chances of some type of virus infecting the entire city except for her was freakishly realistic, scaring her slightly.

It ended up being four in the afternoon when Emily and Brett stumbled out of the arcade, both of them breathing heavily as they'd just finished playing a rhythm game which had required them to flail their legs towards different buttons which were annoyingly far away from each other.

"Café?" Brett questioned, to which Emily nodded, knowing that she needed a coffee.

"Yes," she replied as they began to walk across the road and towards the nearest café.

They entered, ordered a coffee each and sat at a table by the window, both of them staring out of it as they caught their breath back properly and thought.

"It's four," Brett stated, glancing at his phone to check the time.

"Eight more hours," Emily mumbled, feeling drained. Maybe playing that rhythm game hadn't been the best idea given that she needed to stay awake for another eight hours. Well, she didn't *need* to, but she wanted to. It would be safer to be conscious throughout the remainder of the day.

"What's the furthest you've gotten?" Brett questioned, to which Emily shrugged.

"Seven, I think," she replied, unsure. "Maybe a little later."

Brett let out a light sigh. "I'll help for as long as

I can, but I don't know what I'll be able to do."

Emily smiled weakly. "It's fine," she said. "You've done loads already."

Brett shook his head lightly, either denying what Emily had said or reluctant to go home and leave her alone.

"What now, then?" He proceeded to ask, Emily pausing to consider that.

"I suppose I'll just go home and I'll go to bed," she said, Brett seeming to perk up at that slightly before he took a light sip of his coffee.

"I'll walk you home," he said instantly, his tone showing how adamant he was about that idea. "Doing that will let me keep you safe for at least a *little* longer, I hope."

Emily nodded lightly, accepting the offer, slightly relieved that she wouldn't have to make the journey alone.

The two of them spent ten minutes sitting and finishing their drinks before they decided to go. They left the café and began to walk in the direction of Emily's apartment briskly, neither of them wanting to hang around an area for too long out of a light fear that something would go wrong and would end Emily's attempt on the spot.

As they neared Emily's apartment, maybe only a few blocks away, they heard a commotion from around the corner. Slightly concerned, Brett told Emily to wait around the corner while he stuck his head around it, checking to see what was wrong before he pulled his head back, giving Emily a light shrug. The shouting was still going on, but the source of it wasn't within Brett's vision, so he guessed that there was an argument going on in a nearby building and nothing more, signalling for Emily to continue walking.

The shouting seemed to grow in volume before a flurry of deafening bangs rang out, startling both Emily and Brett. They turned to look at the source of the noises, looking down an alleyway, and seeing that there were two police officers and four other people, the six of them pointing their guns at each other. Upon closer inspection, there was another criminal on the ground alongside two other officers.

Emily and Brett immediately turned to run, but footsteps echoed behind them.

"Go!" Came a voice, the word possibly directed at Emily and Brett as they took-off down the street.

More shots rang out before silence.

Brett pulled Emily to the ground, taking cover behind a parked car, the look on his face clearly showing his petrification.

"Has it stopped?" Emily asked after a few moments of silence passed.

Brett didn't say anything in return, instead moving to stick his head around the car to see what was going on.

One of the criminals shot Brett immediately before turning to look at Emily, pointing the gun at her as she tried to scramble to her feet and run in the opposite direction, wanting to throw-up from the sight of Brett dying.

"No witnesses," came from the criminal's mouth before Emily felt a searing pain erupt in the back of her head.

Chapter 13

Emily woke up and let out a strained sigh. She'd died again, and from a bullet, too, just like the previous attempt. That seemed to solidify it for her. Spending time with Brett wasn't the answer to her problems. So, what was? She'd tried spending the day at work, at home, in the city, with Brett... She'd also tried escaping by train, but maybe that wasn't enough. Maybe leaving the city wouldn't fix the problem. Maybe leaving the country would fix the problem.

Emily slid her sleeping mask and her earmuffs from her head before she silenced the vibrating alarm and moved to call her manager.

After going through the excuse of feeling ill again, Emily jumped from her bed and began to pull her clothes on as quickly as possible, then brushed her hair before going to her kitchen to grab breakfast, looking online for the nearest airport as she waited for the bread to turn to toast.

While eating, she found the nearest airport and saw that there were tickets for a short and cheap flight which would get her out of the country, something which made her smile immediately before she quickly finished her toast, not caring that she was risking chocking as she was more fearful about not being able to get to the airport in time.

She booked a ticket as she walked into her room to grab her coat, then rushed out of the apartment. She didn't need luggage. She was just going to catch the flight, land in the other country, get a hotel and wait for the day to end.

Maybe this will be it, Emily wondered as she moved, not wanting to even begin to believe that there was a chance as she didn't want to get her hopes up, though, being honest with herself, she knew that this was the *only* thing which could possibly work. If it didn't, what else could she do? Getting out of the country, literally *escaping* from it was so much more extreme than simply trying to alter her day.

She descended the stairs, stepped onto the street and immediately began to rush in the direction of the airport. The flight was due to leave within two hours, meaning that Emily had about half-an-hour to get to the airport and to have a decent chance of getting through security in time.

It took forty minutes for Emily to arrive at the airport. She could have caught a taxi, but she didn't want to risk it. Knowing her luck, she'd have only gotten into a car crash.

Once Emily had walked into the airport, she quickly checked-in, got her ticket, passed through security and began to wait at her terminal, passing the time on her phone.

It felt strange to be in an airport without any

luggage, Emily noticed, especially when looking around and seeing everyone else with at least one, small bag. She wondered if she looked strange though quickly ignored the thought. It didn't matter what other people thought of her, especially because she was only catching the flight so that she wouldn't die.

The wait continued, dragging time out artificially, making it feel to Emily as if she'd been sitting there for hours upon hours when, in reality, she'd only been there for one hour by the time that the announcement came to tell everyone to queue to board the plane.

Emily stood and strode forwards, wanting to be one of the first people to get onto the plane. She didn't know why, but she had the feeling that she would be safe directly after stepping onto the aircraft, like it was the indestructible, protective bubble which Brett had said would be good for Emily.

Emily had her ticket checked before she was allowed to walk down the long tube which connected the airport to the plane. Taking the first step felt surreal, like she was doing something completely alien to the rest of the human race. She'd even been in a plane before, so the feeling must have only stemmed from the hope that she was on her way to escaping her nightmare.

Once Emily had stepped onto the plane, she smiled widely, looking down the long, long tube of seats. A stewardess informed her that she was seated in F6, motioning for her to go to it before Emily obliged, making her way towards her seat, the smile still plastered on her face.

    She made her way to her seat. She was stationed by the window, something which she didn't mind very much. It was a short flight, so she didn't think that she'd have to get past the people who'd be sat beside her to go to the bathroom.

    It took a few more minutes for two other people to sit on Emily's row, the large amount of the passengers on the aircraft by that time. Emily watched the stewardess as she confirmed that everyone was present after a few moments, signalling for the connecting tube to be disconnected from the plane before she closed the door.

    The stewardess began to go through the regular spiel which she had to do with every flight, giving the debriefing about what to do if an emergency-situation would occur, getting through the explanation within a few minutes before she told everyone to make sure that they were fastened into their seats, wishing them a good flight. She made her way into the cockpit, probably to tell the pilot that it was okay to get into the air.

    The people next to Emily weren't squashing her, something which genuinely surprised Emily a little as being stationed next to a comically-sized person who would suffocate her to death by pushing her against the side of the aircraft was a genuine possibility given that she'd been subjected to so many deaths, some of them having been quite stupid like being badly electrocuted while trying to unplug her TV, and others were completely unfair like stumbling across the police dealing with armed criminals and being killed just because she'd witnessed the ordeal, or even falling onto the train tracks because so many people had decided to catch the same train at the same time. Other times, yes, the deaths had been reasonable. She'd been hit by a car because she hadn't been careful enough, she'd drowned in the bath because she'd fallen asleep in it, she'd ended up burning to death because she'd left an empty, metal pot on top of the stove which she'd forgotten to turn off. So, as there was a clear variety when it came to the fairness of the situations, Emily wouldn't have been surprised had she been killed for another, stupid reason.

The plane was fairly quiet for a few moments before it began to roll down the runway, the aircraft rumbling slightly as the wheels took it across the tarmac, speeding up more and more until it finally left the ground, zooming into the air and towards the destination.

The silence continued for a few moments before a few people started talking, then a few more, then a few more. Some zips could be heard opening, people opening carry-on bags. Emily could see a businessman out of the corner of her eye as he pulled his laptop from his bag, turned it on and began to type something on it a minute later. The noise wasn't too bad, though, simply adding to the ambience.

Emily pushed her head into her headrest, closing her eyes and realising that she hadn't brought her earmuffs of sleeping mask. She'd left the apartment in such a hurry, scared of missing the flight that she hadn't thought about the fact that she'd be spending the night in a different country. She needed them if she was going to sleep but, being honest with herself, Emily doubted that she would. Even if she *would* make it past midnight, she wouldn't trust herself to go to sleep and to wake up in the morning. There was always the chance that she'd die and have to go through the whole thing again, maybe even that she'd have to live the rest of her life like this, going through every single day over and over while trying to survive and live as normally as possible, ignoring the situation. Though, there was also the question of when the ordeal had started. Maybe this *was* normal life, just no-one else had experienced it or spoken about it before. Maybe she'd been incredibly lucky over the nineteen years that she been alive, having gotten through every day on her first attempt without dying.

Or, maybe, as she hoped, the curse would be destroyed at midnight.

A giant rumble struck the jet twenty minutes into the flight, people jolting a little but not thinking much of it, unanimously deciding that it was simply turbulence. Though, when it happened again and again, then a bang could be heard from the outside of the jet, everyone grew slightly scared and curious about what was happening. A mother looked out of the window which was the closest to her and shrieked.

"The left engine!" She yelled, pulling her hands to cover her mouth as if she was on stage and giving a performance. "It's on fire!"

A few people bolted from their seats to look at it, quickly confirming with panicked voices.

The stewardess rushed in to see everyone. "Yes, the left engine had exploded," she explained. Even *she* sounded panicked, and she was supposed to calm everyone down! "We'll be making an emergency landing as soon as possible, so everyone *please* remain in your seats."

"But... we're passing over the sea," an older man said, his petrified face staring at the stewardess as if expecting her to climb onto the wing of the aircraft and to fix the engine.

The stewardess' expression faltered slightly, but she made an extreme effort to keep smiling at them. "Yes, but it's okay!" She reassured. "We'll get to land soon enough. Just *please* stay in your seats and try to remain calm. We'll be fine."

As if the plane had heard the stewardess and wanted to mock her, it began to jolt, rumbling, either turbulence or something else. It continued, the stewardess almost losing her balance, holding herself up with the headrests of the two closest seats until it worsened. The aircraft jolted more and more before another bang was heard, this time originating from the other side of the aircraft.

Emily looked out of her window, trying to think positively about her situation as they'd already left the country, heading towards the destination. She prayed that she wouldn't end up dying, but her heart dropped instantly.

"This engine's blown up, too," she informed everyone, her voice clearly bitter.

Everyone began to panic so much more, the stewardess trying her best to calm everyone, to reassure them that they were going to survive, but even *she* looked petrified.

Then the plane began to jut a little, going up and down, up and down incredibly suddenly. Then it began to tilt towards the sea.

The aircraft jolted as the pilot tried to stabilise it, to lift it up again and to aim it in the direction of land, but their efforts were completely hopeless as the aircraft sped up more and more, accelerating towards the ground, reaching its terminal velocity and not slowing down in the slightest.

Then it hit the water.

The deceleration was enough to kill most of the people on the plane. The front of the aircraft crumpled like a tin can being stepped on, folding in on itself, almost enough to kill Emily though, for the first time since the ordeal had begun, she had been lucky. Maybe getting out of the country *was* helping?

The crumpling of the aircraft had destroyed all of the windows, most of them having been smashed completely, though a few had only been badly cracked. The glass of the window which Emily was sat beside pierced her leg and made her wince, but that was nothing when the sea water began to rush into the plane as it sank lower and lower into the sea.

The saltiness of the water stung Emily's wounds

as it passed, landing at her feet and sliding down the tilted aircraft, making its way towards the lowest part.

Then the water began to fill the aircraft.

With almost all of the windows having been smashed, water seeping through all of them, the aircraft began to fill more and more, and it wasn't slowly.

The people who were alive- which wasn't many- began to scurry to get out of their seats, trying to climb up the slope of the aircraft, trying to get to the nearest door but, once someone had reached the only emergency exit which hadn't been destroyed by the crash, they couldn't open it. The water pressure was too much. Even when three other people made it to the door, they still couldn't push it open.

Some people turned to the windows, seeing if they could squeeze through them, though the windows were too small. The few children who'd survived could fit through with a push, maybe, but then what?

The water continued to fill the aircraft, everyone who wasn't stuck trying to scramble to the highest point of the aircraft, Emily included, almost standing on top of the back of one of the seats.

"What do we do?" A distressed man questioned as if expecting someone to know every single detail about the most optimal escape route.

"I don't know," Emily murmured, feeling all hope leave her body. Maybe leaving the country *did* have an effect. She could have *easily* been killed by the crash, but she hadn't. Still, though, she was going to drown. If there *was* some type of effect which had come from escaping the country, it hadn't done enough to keep her alive.

The water continued to fill the aircraft, metres of space being engulfed by the water within a few seconds.

It didn't take long for the water to surround Emily and the other survivors.

Chapter 14

Emily jolted awake, the burning feeling in her lungs beginning to fade away. She'd died. Again. Even though she'd both hoped and expected that leaving the country would fix her situation, she'd been wrong. It hadn't. Maybe she'd *actually* been unlucky. The fact that she hadn't been killed by the initial crash suggested that she'd managed to evade the curse, or something, but she'd woken up again. Maybe she *would* be safer outside of the country, but there had definitely been something more than bad luck at play during that plane ride. One engine exploding during the journey was unlucky, but both of them? The second one had burst into flames only a minute or two after the first, so that couldn't possibly be the strain of the aircraft only using the right engine, could it?

That solidified it for Emily. Leaving the country wasn't an option. Leaving the city wasn't an option. Using a friend as a safety net wasn't an option. Running away from her normal life wasn't an option. Staying at home wasn't an option. Even getting through her day normally wasn't an option.

She didn't have any other option.

Emily pulled her sleeping mask and her

earmuffs from her head and buried her face in her hands, beginning to sob to herself about the situation. Her alarm vibrated against her chest, but she couldn't even face turning if off. Silencing the alarm would be accepting that she'd just be going into another attempt, and she couldn't face it. She felt drained. She just wanted to be able to relax for however long it was possible to do so, but she knew that she couldn't, and it wasn't as if she was battling against a deadline or as if she'd be busy for the next few days. The problem was that she physically couldn't take a break as she'd just end up dying, and the stress about the knowledge of that was too much to be able to sit in bed for as long as possible. She'd know that she'd have to die again and would be wondering what the cause would be. She wouldn't be in a fit state to relax, she'd be torturing herself, essentially.

Emily remained there for another minute before she silenced her alarm. What could she do? Giving up wasn't an option, so she'd have to try to do something else, but what? She could always catch a different flight, she could always walk out of the city, but Emily doubted that she'd get anywhere. The plane would crash again, she'd be hit by a car, *anything* would happen if it would prevent her from leaving.

She slid from her bed slowly and went to pull her clothes on though, after a moment of considering it, she couldn't even face that. Her body felt as if she'd just sprinted for the entirety of a marathon, her mind felt as if she'd just sat an exam which was designed to test rocket scientists. She couldn't think of anything. It was like a bad case of writer's block, just she wasn't writing a story, she was coming up with an idea as to how to remain alive.

Maybe it would be better to just kneel over and die for real.

Emily paused as she shuffled into the kitchen. What if that was it? What if she needed to die? It sounded insane. She'd been spending so long trying to avoid death that Emily felt like a psychopath for even considering the possibility of allowing herself to die, but there was a reason behind her thought process: trying to survive wasn't working. She'd always end up dying in the end and having to restart the day, so trying to die would have the opposite effect, maybe? Maybe she could commit suicide, then she'd wake up the next day and everything would be back to normal? Though, of course, there was the idea that giving in would kill her permanently though, when being honest with herself, Emily guessed that it would probably be better to die than to have to torment herself with her situation. Maybe it would be better for her.

She flopped onto the couch, considering it more. Was it really going to be the answer? Would she wake up with everything back to normal, or would it have the same effect as every other death? Was she *really* trapped in the death-loop until she could survive for the entire day, or was there a chance of breaking out? Even then, was there a chance that breaking out would be permanent death? Maybe she'd already died and this situation was her brain needing to accept that... What if *that* was the truth?

Emily felt ill. She'd never considered suicide in her life. She'd been lucky. She'd never suffered from any type of mental illness- at least excluding what the situation had undoubtedly thrust upon her- so the thought of being the one to inflict the pain...

She stood up shakily. She didn't have another idea. Escaping the country had been so promising, yet it hadn't worked, so would *any* of her attempts work? If she didn't at least try, she'd probably be subjected to the loop forever. What did she have to lose?

Emily began to make her way towards the kitchen, pulling a drawer open when she'd reached it, removing a knife. She'd slit her throat. That's what she'd do. It would be quick, right? It would hurt for a few seconds, but she'd die quickly, right? The thought of running in front of a car crossed her mind, though Emily disregarded it. She'd been hit by a car before and that had been the start of the loop. While it seemed poetic for the possible last death to be the same one which had started it, Emily didn't expect that it would do anything. Maybe she had to die in a specific way, like jumping from a great height, hanging herself, stabbing herself, overdosing, something like that. Being hit by a car but not being freed even though it would be willingly would convince her that her idea had failed even if she was on the right track, and that was something which Emily didn't want to have to face. Getting up from the couch and picking up the knife had been hard enough.

She didn't want to have to kill herself twice.

Emily stared at the blade. She almost felt upset while looking at it. She felt like she was coming to the end of a story which she loved, like she was on the last, tiny chapter of a book series which had been with her for her entire life, like she was about to watch the last episode of a show which she loved. Like she was about to end her story.

Her hand lowered a little. She didn't want to do it. She wasn't suicidal, but did she have a choice? Not really, when thinking about it. If she'd avoid it, she'd never know if it was the solution...

She hated what she'd have to do. Emily knew that suicide wasn't the answer for a lot of things- for anything, even- but for her, maybe it would be? But, even looking at the knife, she almost felt guilty. So many people would end their lives due to suffering, whether that would be as a result of depression or something else, but Emily would be doing it to benefit her? At least somewhat? It just felt wrong to her, like she would be making light of something so dark and so real.

But she had to do it.

Emily held the knife to her throat, her breathing steadily increasing. It wasn't bad when she'd die via every other way. Most of the time, she hadn't been expecting it. But here, she'd know when it would happen. She knew that it was about to happen. She had no type of filter to prevent the fear running through her mind. What if this was it? What if she would die

permanently as a result of her actions?
    Doing her best to disregard her thoughts, Emily slashed at herself with the knife.

Chapter 15

The doctor's pace quickened as he rushed through the hallways of the hospital. He'd just been told that one of his patients was experiencing worryingly abnormal heartrate behaviour, something which scared him, made him think that something was wrong inside of the patient's body, and so he rushed as fast as he could without sprinting as he didn't want to startle everybody else, especially as he was heading through the cardiac ward.

He passed a few colleagues but, of course, didn't stop to talk. After turning to the left and seeing that the hallway was almost empty, he decided to throw caution to the wind and to quicken his pace ever-so-slightly. It probably wasn't anything to worry about *too* much, but it wasn't normal. It definitely wasn't normal, that being what scared him.

Poor girl, he thought as he rushed around another corner, having to slow a little to avoid another doctor who was wheeling a patient towards somewhere unknown. *As if she hasn't been through enough already.*

It took another minute or two for him to turn around the corner and to look at the sleeping face of Emily Parr, her nose connected to a tube which was connected to a machine to help to regulate her breathing, her arm connected to an IV which was feeding her the nutrients which she needed.

Emily was in a coma. After the car had hit her, she'd been rushed to the hospital and had been in the comatose state ever since. Her heartrate had heightened and lowered occasionally, though, as the doctor stared at the monitor, he couldn't believe what he was seeing. Her heartrate was much, much higher than it *should* be for anyone in a coma. Of course, she was probably dreaming, but the rate was increasing more and more. It was slow, but the incline was noticeable. If it would get too high...

There was another doctor in the room, trying her best to fix the problem. She glanced up at him and shrugged in a semi-panicked manner, unsure as to what to do. It seemed as if she'd already tried many different techniques, but nothing seemed to be working.

He stared at Emily, trying to figure out what was going on in her head which had sparked a giant flux of heartrate. Maybe it was some type of nightmare which she was stuck in, unable to get out of as she was suffering from her coma? But, then again, the head injury which she'd sustained from her skull slamming into the concrete of the road would surely have affected *something*. Maybe every dream was unpleasant. Maybe she was reliving the accident over and over again like having to sit in front of the TV and watch the same scene of a film over and over and over and over again. It would be maddening to do that, he knew, so he couldn't bear to think about what it must have felt like for Emily if that was, in fact, what she was experiencing.

Or, maybe, she didn't know that she was experiencing the same thing over and over again. Maybe she was simply suffering from a bad case of déjà vu.

Printed in Great Britain
by Amazon